"Kira, you can't ignore this and make it go away."

"You keep saying you know what I'm going through," Kira said. "You can't know. You can't know how it felt to be trapped in that car with a lunatic after me," she insisted. "I thought I was fine, but when I got home..."

"The shadows start talking, don't they?"

She was afraid to look at him and let him know he was right. "I can't tell my family what happened, Dallas."

"You're probably going to be mad at me, because I told your brothers what happened, so they'd understand my concerns that your condo looked suspicious and stop acting like this was a lover's spat. They thought I broke your heart. Right about now, I wish it *was* just a personal fight between us."

"What?"

Dallas took hold of her hand. "Because then you wouldn't be hearing the shadows talking. Because then we wouldn't have so much in common. Because then I wouldn't be afraid for your safety."

Books by Carol Steward

Love Inspired Suspense

Gurdian of Justice #83

Love Inspired

There Comes a Season #27
Her Kind of Hero #56
Second Time Around #92
Courting Katarina #134
This Time Forever #165
Finding Amy #263
Finding Her Home #282
Journey to Forever #301

*In the Line of Fire

CAROL STEWARD

To Carol Steward, selling a book is much like riding a roller coaster—every step of the process, every sale, brings that exhilarating high. During the less exciting times, she's busy gathering ideas and refilling her cup. Writing brings a much-needed balance to her life, as she has her characters share lessons she has learned, as well.

When she's not working at the University of Northern Colorado, you can usually find her spending time with her husband of over thirty years, writing and thanking God she survived raising her own three children to reap His rewards of playing with her adorable grandchildren.

Throughout all of the different seasons of life, God has continued to teach Carol to turn to Him. She has also learned to simplify her life and appreciate her many blessings—His gift of creativity, sharing her love for God with readers and setting an example of what God can do when we say, "Yes, God, take me, shape me, use me." To find out more about Carol's slightly crazy life and her books, visit her Web site at www.carolsteward.com.

CAROL STEWARD

GUARDIAN *of* JUSTICE

Steeple
Hill®

Published by Steeple Hill Books™

STEEPLE HILL BOOKS

Steeple
Hill®

ISBN-13: 978-0-373-44273-7
ISBN-10:   0-373-44273-4

GUARDIAN OF JUSTICE

Copyright © 2008 by Carol Steward

www.SteepleHill.com

Printed in U.S.A.

Paul wrote, "The one thing I do...is to forget what is behind me and do my best to reach what is ahead.
—*Philippians* 3:13

Many thanks for making this series possible go to my editor, Melissa Endlich. I couldn't have gotten through this without you. To my critique partners, Maya and Noelle, and my husband and kids for helping me to keep going through this challenge.

I'd like to thank the dedicated law enforcement officers and their families and pray for their safety. I also want to acknowledge my appreciation to David Galyard for his help, and to my father for inspiring my admiration and respect for the men in uniform. And to my son Matt who surprised me and became a guardian of justice. And to his wife and family, God bless and stay safe out there!

ONE

"Kira Matthews?" The officer at the window of the Police Station motioned her forward. "You'll be riding with Dallas Brooks tonight. He needs to pick you up right outside these doors. If you'll go on out, he'll be here in a few minutes."

"Thanks," Kira said as she hurried out the doors to wait. A cruiser pulled to a stop in front of the station and the driver yelled, "If you're Kira Matthews, get in."

She nodded. "Nice to meet—"

"Sorry to rush you, I just got called out."

She quickly climbed into the car and set her tote bag on the floor. "What's the call?"

"Someone dialed 911, then hung up. Not a good way to start a Friday night."

"I know what you mean." Kira buckled her seat belt and Dallas took off, lights on and siren blaring. She held tight to the grab bar above the passenger's door of the squad car, trying to keep her balance. "You take 911 hang-ups pretty seriously. It doesn't take more than a few minutes to get anywhere in Antelope Springs. After all, we're not in Denver. I'm sorry I was late arriving. I had an unexpected call from a foster parent right as I was leaving at five o'clock."

"No problem. The dispatcher heard yelling in the background before whoever it was hung up, so I don't want to waste any time. If it's a prank, I'd like to catch the kid and teach him not to cry wolf." As the officer turned the corner to Sixth Street, he cut the lights and siren on the squad car. "I'm Dallas Brooks, by the way." Pulling to a stop diagonally across the end of the driveway, he glanced quickly at her. "Stay in the car. If it is a viable domestic call, guns or knives are always a possibility."

"But I'm a social worker," she started to say.

"Good, that may come in handy. Even more reason to keep you out of harm's way." He gave her a quick smile and turned off the engine. "I'll let you know when it's safe to come in, all right?"

"I walk into houses unarmed on a regular basis, Officer. We handle these calls every day, all day, just like you do. Dispatch said there may be kids in the house, and I should be there."

"And if there are, I'll come get you when I know if it's necessary and if it's safe." He climbed out of the car, closing the door on her next words.

"Humph," she muttered. Kira watched Officer

Brooks study the situation as he walked up the driveway. When he reached the front of the house, she opened her door. Just as she put her foot on the asphalt, she heard a loud bang, yelling, and glass breaking. She jumped out of the vehicle and started toward the house.

"Get back in the car," Dallas ordered. He pointed to the cruiser. "I don't need to worry about you, too," he said in a loud whisper, before putting his hand on his gun and stepping to the side of the entry. He knocked on the door and announced his presence, glancing in her direction again.

Kira moved hesitantly back to the car and turned her attention to the police radio. It didn't take long for Officer Brooks to call dispatch for backup. "I hope you have the sense to wear your vest," she muttered, feeling a sudden pang of anxiety at the thought.

It was warm for a spring evening and Kira wished she had the courage to turn the key and open the windows. If the sun wasn't disappearing so quickly, she would. It would be just her luck the call would be nothing and the officer would come right out. Fanning herself with a notepad, Kira propped her door open with her leg to let some fresh air inside.

She heard a rattling sound and searched for the source. To the side of the house, a man had just jumped the gate in a chain-link fence and was staggering toward the car ahead of the cruiser. *I hope he realizes we're blocking the driveway,* she thought. He started to get in, then saw the police car. Ducking behind the other vehicle, he studied the house. He seemed undecided whether to keep his eye on the cruiser or the building as he crawled along the half-dead, creeping juniper bushes edging the driveway. He kept turning his head back and forth, as if watching to make sure Officer Brooks didn't come out and catch him. He brushed his long bushy hair back as he stepped around a bicycle in the driveway and moved toward the driver's side of the patrol car.

Surely he wasn't thinking of taking it, she thought. Kira pulled her leg into the car and quietly closed the door, searching for an automatic door lock. *Where is it?*

As soon as he was past the tallest juniper, the man charged toward the cruiser. Kira dived across the seat, pressing the lock button on the driver's door just as the creepy guy tried to open it. He had tattoos, she noted, and his T-shirt was torn and spattered with blood.

He slammed his fist against the window and swore. Then he slumped across the hood, pressed his face to the windshield and locked his attention on Kira. Blood dripped from his forehead.

Her heart raced. *Sure, stay in the car where it's safe. Thanks a lot, Officer Brooks.*

The madman stared at her for long moments, his eyes full of rage. He had to be high on something.

"God, stop this man before he hurts anyone else," Kira prayed aloud. "Keep me safe, and the officer, too."

Finally, sliding off the car, he turned and disappeared among the shadows of the trees near the front entrance.

Why is he going into the house? Kira grabbed the radio receiver and pressed the button, just as she'd always wanted to do when she sat in her father's patrol car as a child. "Help!" Suddenly, the radio codes she'd heard so many times vanished into thin air. She could practically visualize them as if they were written on paper, but for the life of her she couldn't think of the one she needed. "Dispatch, this is Kira Matthews," she finally said. The man had appeared again, and was bending over in front of the house to pick something up.

"What are you doing on this channel?" a voice answered. The dispatcher obviously wasn't used to distress calls from ride-alongs.

"Send help," she yelped, dropping the mike when she saw the man heading back toward her, waving a huge rock above his head.

Panic pulsed through her. She found the mike again and forced herself to speak slowly. "I'm a...a social worker riding along with..." What was his name? "Brooks," she blurted, then screamed as the crazy man heaved the rock at the driver's door, shaking the squad car. "A man is trying to break into the cruiser. Help!"

Dispatch didn't respond.

The man threw the rock at the car again, barely missing the window this time. The rock bounced onto the hood and he followed it.

Kira gulped. He was going to get in unless she did something. She searched fervently for controls for the lights and sirens.

"Oh come on, where are they?" She leaned closer to the dash in her search.

As the man stood up on the hood of the car, he threw the rock directly at her. Kira reached out and hit the horn.

TWO

Dallas approached the modest brick house, taking mental notes. *Small basement windows. Tall juniper bushes block the view from street to front door. The edge of a curtain is caught in the closed window. Where's the screen?* He stepped closer and looked around, wondering if he'd missed it on the ground nearby. The other windows each had them. Why not this one? He glanced at the front door again, then the window. Dallas heard a loud bang and reached for his gun as glass shattered.

A deep voice yelled profanities. Doors slammed, as if someone was leaving. Someone madder than a raging bull. Dallas stepped back into the driveway, around the junky old car, and took a look around the corner of the house to get his bearings. A heavy padlock secured the chain-link gate to the backyard. Junk was piled on the other side. He listened, but didn't hear any sounds of movement. He had a sudden image of being back in the high school the day of the shooting.

Inside, a woman's voice bellowed, "You just had to torque him off, didn't you? I don't know how you think we're going to come up with the money to fix that window!"

"Same way you pay for everything else, I 'spect," a young boy snapped back, a slight crack in his voice.

Dallas heard the sound of skin slapping skin. It didn't sound like a prank call any longer. He glanced toward the cruiser. Looked like Kira Matthews was going to be working tonight, after all. She was already on her way.

"Get back in the car," he said as quietly as he could, waving her away. She took her own sweet time following his order, he noted. He crept up the steps and to the side of the entrance.

"PD 138 requesting backup ASAP. Domestic disturbance in progress."

"Copy 138."

"One-ten responding," Mark Pierson replied.

Dallas knocked on the door, ready to announce his presence, just as the woman blasted the child with enough profanity to burn even his jaded ears.

"Police, open the door," he yelled.

The woman murmured something that he couldn't make out, then yelled, "Hold yer horses."

Dallas heard faint footsteps run on hard floors inside the house. "Police. Open the door," he repeated. He rested one hand on his gun and the other on the handle of the screen door. He pressed the button and pulled. *Locked.* "Ma'am, open the door, now."

He heard three locks click before the wood door opened, then one more click opened the screen. The residents were afraid of anyone getting in, that was for sure. In most neighborhoods, two locks were overly cautious. In this subdivision, three was definitely overkill. A padlocked gate and heavily secured door? Something wasn't right.

"Yeah?" The woman who appeared pulled the door closed behind her, blocking his view of the inside.

He nodded toward the house. "We had a 911 call from this residence. I'm going to need to come in and make sure everything is okay, ma'am."

"No one here called you." She glanced behind her and muttered another profanity before returning her attention to Dallas. "My kid just broke that window and I lost my temper. Ya know, kids don't have any respect these days." Her speech slurred and she tugged her stringy blond hair away from her pocked face. "It's no big deal. I mean yelling, ya just gotta do it sometimes with fifteen-year-olds." The woman's hands didn't stop moving in random jerky gestures.

Keep her calm, she's on some sort of drugs. "I'm going to need to talk to everyone, make sure you've all calmed down before I can leave."

There was a long pause before she opened the door and motioned him inside. "See? The kid is fine."

Dallas looked around as he stepped in, adrenaline causing a pulsing in his temples. He had a bad feeling. Just like the day in the school. "Is there anyone else in the house?"

She got a panicked look on her gaunt face. "I don't want no trouble, Officer." Her head twitched as she spoke.

Dallas took another step inside. A gangly boy stood, barefoot, in the middle of the broken glass, glaring at his mother. "Who was slamming doors when I walked up the steps?" Dallas asked.

No one said a word. Everything seemed quiet elsewhere in the house. Was it too quiet? He glanced down the hall toward the next room. There were no lights on, no sounds.

Pulling a small pad of paper and a pen from his chest pocket, Dallas jotted down a few notes for the report. "I need your name," he said with his pen poised.

She threw her head back and crossed her arms over her chest as she let out a groan. "Shirley Mason."

He heard dialogue from dispatch coming through the radio on his shoulder and turned it down slightly so it didn't interrupt his discussion with the family.

Dallas shot a quick glance at the boy. Drops of red on the floor next to the window caught his eye as he did so. "And this young man is your son?" he asked.

The woman nodded.

"Your name?" Dallas asked the teenager.

After a short pause, the boy answered, "Cody."

"Last name?"

"Jones," Cody said.

"What happened here?" Dallas asked him.

"I just told you what happened. You got more questions, ask me," Shirley ordered, making it clear that she'd do the talking.

Dallas looked at Cody's bare feet and the shards of glass surrounding them. "You cut?" Something didn't add up here. Dallas lifted the boy out of the glass, noting the lack of meat on his ribs.

Cody shook his head. "I'm fine," he said, with obvious satisfaction at disobeying his mother. Her glare was lethal.

"So who's bleeding?" The child he'd heard running had sounded much smaller. Was that who'd been cut? Could that be who'd slammed the doors? A sibling, maybe? Was Cody trying to protect a brother or sister? "Ma'am, please go sit on the sofa while we sort through all of this." He checked the boy for cuts while the mother stomped over and dropped onto the shabby couch.

"Who else is or was in the house?"

No answer. Over the mike, Dallas heard broken messages from a frantic voice. Why in the world wasn't dispatch intervening? He didn't need a distraction right now, he thought, as he turned the volume down even more.

The beeping of a car horn sounded. *What's going on now?* He went to the door to see what was happening, and noticed the lights of his cruiser flashing. Then the siren started, drilling through the brick walls.

"Don't either of you move an inch!" Dallas said as he rushed out the door. He jumped off the porch in time to see a man running down the street.

Dallas looked frantically for the social worker. "Miss Matthews?" He turned and scanned behind him, then spun back to the car. *Where is she?*

Again he radioed dispatch. "We have a suspect fleeing a domestic disturbance. He's headed south on Sixth Street, toward Main Street. Long dark hair, medium build, average height, jeans and white T-shirt. There are three, possibly more subjects here at the house."

He couldn't see Miss Matthews in the car, but the doors were still closed. And the passenger half of the windshield was shattered like a spider web.

"Subject may have vandalized a police cruiser," he reported. He looked down the street again, then scanned the area between the car and the road, seeing nothing. He leaned closer to the cruiser and finally saw her lying across the seat with her hands over her head. *She's hurt!* He realized. The adrenaline pulsing through his body came screeching to a sudden halt.

Mark Pierson's police car rushed past the house and took off after the suspect while Dallas tried to open his cruiser's door.

It wasn't closed tight, but it was locked. He knocked repeatedly. "Miss Matthews, open the door." When she jumped, she hit her head on the steering wheel. She turned toward him, rubbing her temple. Her huge eyes shone with fright as she fumbled for the door handle.

"Are you okay?" Dallas reached across and turned off the siren and lights, then backed out of the car again. She was shaking. He quickly took stock, glad to see that the broken windshield had held. The majority of the damage was right in front of the passenger. He shook her gently. "Miss Matthews?"

"Stay in the car, out of harm's way, my foot!" She pointed to the windshield and started to climb out, but Dallas stopped her.

He touched his hand to her shoulder and knelt down between the door and the car. "Hang on there for a minute. Tell me what happened." Kira's cocoa-colored skin seemed paler than it had before the incident. Was she in shock?

"What happened? Didn't you hear me telling dispatch?" Wide-eyed, he gazed darted from the shattered windshield to him.

The frantic voice made sense now. "A little, but it wasn't really clear," he said, not about to admit she'd sounded like a lunatic. He hadn't even realized it was her speaking. Now he at least understood why.

She was going through everything that had happened when as another officer approached. Pete Ford paused, listening.

"You're sure he wanted to get in in order to take the car?" Pete asked.

The social worker glared at him. "Look at the driver's door! It has to have a dent the size of…" She glanced at her hand, then at Dallas's. "The size of your fist," she said, grabbing his wrist and lifting it in the air.

Pete walked around the car and nodded. "Yep, it sure does."

"And when he couldn't get in, he must have decided I could be convinced to let him in, for he threw the rock at the door again and again. He obviously wasn't thinking about safety glass." She shivered.

When Miss Matthews had finished talking, Pete pointed to the house. "Who's inside? I'll catch up there."

"Mom and a son. Shirley—" Dallas glanced at his notes "—Mason, and Cody Jones. I suspect there's a younger child, but no one is talking yet. This guy must have been leaving the back of the house as I was going in—"

"He jumped the fence about three to five minutes after you went inside," Miss Matthews confirmed.

Dallas waited a minute to make sure she was through. "I think we need to get that cleared up right away, find out what he was doing here. The suspect I saw running had dark hair—"

"It was past his shoulders," Miss Matthews interrupted again. "And frizzy. Wild looking…" She held her hands a few inches from her head to show how full the guy's hair was. "He was Caucasian. And had tattoos all over his arms." Dallas's mind drifted and he wondered if he had sounded as frazzled after the shooting that day.

Dallas glanced at her hair. From the looks of it, her own would frizz out just as far if it wasn't in a ponytail at the nape of her neck. Her brown eyes were huge, with long lashes framing them. Her gaze darted back to the car, as if it would bite her.

"He was high or stoned, one of the two. His eyes were…scary." She looked back at the windshield and wrapped her arms around herself. "He was bleeding. He put his hands and face up against the glass, so you can probably get fingerprints." She pointed. "Don't let anyone touch that spot."

"We'll take care of that, don't worry." Dallas focused his attention on Kira, wishing he could have prevented this incident. He realized she was processing the experience, a bit at a time. Normally, he'd have been irritated with her for interrupting him, but he understood her shock. He'd been there. He moved to the trunk, popped it open and pulled out a blanket, forcing his post traumatic stress symptoms from his mind, only allowing it to help him prevent her from experiencing a delayed reaction as he had.

Returning, he unfolded it and offered it to her. "Why don't you cover up with this for a few minutes and rest. We'll talk more in a few minutes."

She needed to know someone was there to let her talk.

Thank you. I don't know why I'm so cold."

Dallas knew that soon she'd realize she did know why, she just didn't want to admit it. She wanted to be in control, just like she was every other day. A strong woman like her walked into domestic disturbances on a regular basis, but after tonight, things would be different. "Go on in, I'll be a few more minutes," Dallas said to the other officer. He couldn't bring himself to walk out on Kira yet.

Pete nodded and went inside without a word. Dallas liked knowing the men serving next to him here in the middle of rural Colorado. Pete had a wife and a one-year-old son. That was more than Dallas had known about most of the officers in Phoenix.

He looked into the cruiser, surprised to see Miss Matthews had leaned her head back and closed her eyes. He knew her calm wouldn't last very long.

More officers showed up, and he let them assist in the search for evidence, and keep spectators off the premises while they finished the investigation. He assigned one officer to find out what neighbors knew about the family.

Dallas took the opportunity to take notes for his report. About ten minutes later he noticed Miss Matthews's eyes were open again, and he leaned back into the car. "Are you warming up?"

She nodded. "I thought for a minute that he was going to go into the house after you. I couldn't think of anything to do except pray and honk the horn, hoping maybe that would scare him away."

Dallas reached for her hand and held on tight. He

wished he could give her the strength to get through the evening unscathed. "You did a great job. I like your quick thinking. Take a deep breath and be thankful that it wasn't any worse."

THREE

"Are there kids inside?" Kira didn't dare dwell on what had happened. She needed to help the children get away from this crazy man. There wasn't time to waste. Kira couldn't believe Dallas wasn't back inside the house yet. Why was he still out here? And why wouldn't he let her go in?

"Yeah, but you're not going in yet." He kept jotting notes, looking around, talking to other officers and jotting more. From the firm set of his jaw and shoulder, she knew he wouldn't be easy to convince. He kept his emotions carefully guarded.

She knew from her brothers' comments that officers had to secure the premises before allowing anyone into a volatile scene. What were the chances that Kira would have ended up in the line of fire while waiting outside? "It couldn't be any worse inside, could it? We have a job to do."

"It's getting done. You need to calm down."

"I am calm," she argued.

"Yeah, I see that." One side of his mouth turned up. It wasn't quite a smile, but maybe he was one of those brooding types that didn't smile. "Calm down some more, then." He quirked an eyebrow, revealing a sense of humor in his blue eyes.

Kira looked around at the half-dozen officers who were making their presence known in the neighborhood. "I will point out I followed your orders to a T. Am I supposed to be a robot and not get a bit riled after being scared out of my wits?" That's all it was, she reassured herself. It was no more frightening than when her brothers jumped out at her from around the corner in the dark basement.

But it *was* different, her ugly conscience reminded her. This wasn't in the security of her adopted family's basement. This was….

She wasn't going to let herself think about it. Not now.

"I need to get in there, Officer Brooks. The last place I should be is out here twiddling my thumbs."

"We'll go, in a few minutes. I just know it's too soon to jump right back into the middle of the situation. A little more time wouldn't be a bad idea. We're trained to always prepare for the unexpected when responding to a domestic disturbance, but…" Dallas cleared his throat. "I shouldn't have…" He couldn't even think of what he'd done wrong. It was just a bad situation.

"I'm not blaming you." She felt bad for razzing him

now. She hadn't expected him to take it personally. His sensitivity caught her off guard, and she felt the warmth of his hand holding hers all over again. "The guy could have come barreling out of the back room of the house," she said quietly. The last thing Dallas needed right now was for the other officers to hear her comforting him. "You didn't know. If Child Protection had received the call, I'd have been here without a police escort at all." She needed to take her mind off how handsome Dallas was and get back to work. "For now, could I at least get out of this car?"

He paused just long enough to make her wonder whether something else was happening. He gave a quick scan of the area, then moved out of her way. He took the blanket as it fell from her shoulders, and wrapped it around her again. "It's getting a little chilly. Why don't you keep this with you?" His gaze lingered a moment too long before he broke the connection. She knew it was dangerous to let her feelings show and to let herself read anything into Dallas's gaze.

Kira stretched and shook her legs out, as if she'd been cramped in the car for ages. They had left the station a little over an hour ago.

She walked around the car and saw the gouge in the door where the sharp rock had dented the steel. "If the crazy guy hadn't been so high, he probably would have hit his target."

"Yeah," Dallas responded somberly. "Remember not

to touch the car anymore. We've called for an investigator to come get prints. Do you need anything?"

She shook her head.

"Listen, I have to get back inside and talk to the mother. I want to get a little more information about the situation before I bring you in and frighten them with Child Protection. It's nothing personal."

She regarded him with a speculative gaze. Somehow it felt personal. "Just make sure someone's out here with me, and I'll be fine." She felt another chill go up her spine, and wrapped her arms across her chest, tugging the blanket tighter. "Officer…"

"Dallas."

Yeah, it definitely felt personal. Kira stuffed the attraction deeper inside. She didn't want another cop in her life. Her dad and three brothers were enough. "I'm sorry I broke protocol, with the radio and everything."

"Don't worry about it. You did the right thing," he said quietly.

His clear blue eyes were full of life and pain, yet she saw warmth there, too. He forced a tight-lipped smile before turning away. He was solidly built, but didn't seem to have that tough-guy mentality, as she had initially presumed. Kim realized she was staring, and nodded.

"Officer Williams will stay out here with you to watch for the guy, though I doubt he'll return tonight." Dallas gently patted her arm, and Kira noticed a hint of a smile. "It's going to be okay."

She tried sitting in the cruiser again, but couldn't shake the edginess. How long would it be before she'd forget the madman's eyes staring her down? Kira got back out and leaned against the front fender, watching the house like an anxious puppy.

To the left, two officers visited, pointing down the block. Did they see someone? Other than a few neighbors peering out their darkened windows to see what was happening, all appeared quiet again.

Officer Williams kept his distance, but several times asked if she was doing okay. She jotted notes to be used in her study and glanced up, hoping Dallas would emerge. She was getting worried. She studied the house, wondering what was going on inside.

Behind a round bush, a light appeared suddenly, as if it had risen out of the ground. Kira shrugged the blanket off and dropped it on the grass. She stepped closer, examining the foundation of the house for windows. Keeping her distance from any shadowed areas where someone could be lurking, she stepped past the corner of the house, but the light was gone. Were officers searching the basement? Why were the other windows not lit?

Suddenly, Kira spotted a little girl's face in the glow of the streetlight. A curly haired blonde was peering out of a basement window. Frightened eyes looked around suspiciously, then disappeared. Seconds later a tattered stuffed animal flew from the window well. Kira watched for a moment.

Dallas obviously didn't know the little girl was there, or she'd probably be in a bigger hurry to get out of the house. Officer Williams was busy searching the front yard for evidence. Even if the police did know she was in the house, Kira reasoned, if the child slipped out the small window, they might not be able to catch her. *I'm doing him a favor.*

She hurried forward and offered her hand. "Hi there. I'm Kira Matthews. Do you need some help?"

The little girl dropped back into the house as if she was on a park slide.

How'd she do that? Kira couldn't believe her eyes. The child had disappeared in an instant. Kira hesitantly stepped closer, then knelt down and peered into the dark basement. "It's okay, honey, I can help you. I'm with Social Services. Are you okay?"

"Un-huh," a small voice answered, so quietly Kira could hardly hear her.

She kicked back into her social worker role. "Are you hurt?" When there was no answer, she asked the girl's name. Kira felt her chills return.

She heard scuffling from inside the basement. After a long pause, the girl finally answered, "Betsy."

"That's a really pretty name. How old are you, Betsy?" She heard soft sniffles. The little girl was frightened.

"Betsy, can you come back up here so we can talk?" Kira asked. She wanted to get out of these shadows before the madman returned. With the light beaming out of the basement, she felt as if she had a spotlight trained on her.

Nothing but whimpers broke the silence.

"Can you tell me why you are sneaking out of the house, Betsy?"

"Mama told me to," she whimpered.

Kira waited patiently. She studied the small window, wondering if there was any way she could get through it. Her better judgment warned her not to go into a house blind. Her brothers would never let her live it down if she did. She had no idea what or who would be waiting when and if she finally squeezed through the tiny opening. And by the time she made it, who knew where Betsy would be?

"What happened?"

"Mickey hurt me, so Cody…" She choked up and couldn't talk.

"What did Cody do?"

"He got mad at Mickey, and—" The noise of a motorcycle roaring down the quiet street drowned out her words. "—bat and broke the window. And Mama told me to scat."

Kira recalled the time her brothers had run through the sliding door playing football, and how upset her mother had been. *Hiding makes perfect sense to me, but…* "Mamas get mad sometimes, don't they? Did you say Cody was mad at Mickey?"

"Yep. Mickey's mean. He's a bad dude."

Kira glanced around the yard, certain that Mickey was the crazy man who'd scared her. Kira leaned closer to the basement window and looked inside. She didn't hear anyone else in the background, but saw a soft glow coming through a doorway—likely the source or the light? "Betsy, are you alone in the basement?"

"Yep, I locked the secret door."

Secret door? Kira looked harder, getting as close as she could without sticking her head in the window well. She couldn't see much, and felt for cobwebs. It felt clear.

She eased even closer to the window well and finally ducked her head in, bracing herself against the brick house. There weren't just lights in the other room, there were plants. Lots of them, from what she could tell. "Was Mickey coming after you?" She tried to keep her focus on the little girl and still per around inside. *If it wasn't so bright in the other room, I could see her better.* "Betsy, I want to help you. Come on out."

"Mama be mad," Betsy said with a catch in her voice.

Kira didn't miss things like that. "I'll talk to your mama for you. I want to help you and Cody."

She was met with silence again.

She waited several minutes before she went on. "Betsy, I know you're scared. Together we'll find a way to help you and Cody. I won't let anyone hurt you." She picked up the bear the child had thrown out. "What is your teddy bear's name, Betsy?"

Kira waited, and finally she heard movement. And

then a little blond head again appeared in the opening. The child looked around before climbing out to Kira, hesitating as if she had second thoughts.

"It's okay, Betsy. I'm going to help you." The little girl's eyes reflected not only sadness, but fear and neglect. Kira's heart ached. "Here you go, Betsy. Your teddy missed you."

The little girl snatched the bear from Kira's grip. "Fuzzy."

FOUR

"Miss Matthews?" Dallas paused. "Williams, where's my ride-along? I told you to watch out for her."

Kira started to answer, but one look at the fear on Betsy's face told her to wait. The child was Kira's priority now. "Come here, Betsy. It's okay. I'll make sure you're safe."

"She was next to the car just a minute ago," the other officer answered.

Dallas didn't sound happy, a fact she could hear in his voice even from the other side of the house. "Kira!"

Betsy started to run, but Kira caught her.

"*We're* back here," she said quickly, then glanced at Betsy. "It's okay, honey. It's not Mickey. This is a police officer. He won't hurt you."

Dallas rushed around the corner of the home, then came to an abrupt halt. "Oh, there you are."

Betsy let out a squeal, and Kira wrapped her arm around the little girl. "It's okay." Dallas was tall, with broad shoulders, a menacing sight with the glow of the streetlight behind him. He must look frightening to such a petite girl. Kira let go of Betsy, stood up and offered her hand instead. The little girl shied away when Dallas looked down at her. Betsy clung to her ragged bear…what was left of it.

Kira grasped the child's shoulder. "It's okay, Betsy, Officer Brooks is our friend. He's going to help you, and Cody, too. Aren't you, Officer Brooks?"

Dallas's blue eyes met hers, and Kira felt his anger fade. He reminded her of her oldest brother, Kent. Strong and stubborn. But when it came to kids, she could see his soft side.

"Yeah, we've been worried about you, Betsy. We couldn't find you." He knelt down several feet away and smiled at the little girl. "Did you dial 911 for help?"

Betsy tightened her grip and shook her head, inching behind Kira.

"It's okay if you did. It was very smart to call. And we came here to help you. Betsy, did you get any scratches from the broken window?" he asked gently. Kira realized that with his military haircut, Dallas looked a little like a teddy bear, with a stocky body and full face shadowed with dark stubble.

The little girl kept moving farther away, spinning Kira around in the process. As soon as Betsy realized she was face-to-face with Dallas again, she ducked behind Kira once more.

"I'm going to stay right here. I won't come any closer. Can you show Miss Matthews your arms so we can make sure you're okay?"

Betsy showed one arm while keeping a death grip on Kira, then switched.

Dallas gave a smile of approval. "Thanks, Betsy. Could you answer a few questions for me?"

The frightened child nodded, peeking out from behind Kira.

"Do you know if Cody was playing baseball tonight?"

She shook her head.

"You don't know?" Dallas prompted.

"No, he wasn't playing baseball," Betsy said softly.

Dallas glanced at her bear, then back at her. "What was Cody doing?"

"He was mad at Mickey," she whispered, repeating the story of Mickey hurting her, so Cody took a swing at him with the bat. "I don't like Mickey. Cody don't, neither."

Officer Brooks glanced at Kira, obviously sharing her concern. "Did Mickey hurt you, Betsy?" Kira asked.

Betsy immediately shook her head. Her response was almost too quick.

"If he's hurting you, or your brother, or your mom, Betsy, you need to tell Miss Matthews so we can make sure he doesn't anymore."

Betsy turned away.

"Let's go back into the house. We can talk more later."

Dallas hadn't missed the child's body language,

either, Kira noted. She watched the interaction with admiration. She didn't have fond memories of the officer
who'd taken her and her younger half-brother Jimmy
away after her parents' car accident. And she would
never forget the night Jimmy's family had taken him
away, leaving her with the foster family. Which was
half the reason she was here tonight. It was time
someone made Protective Services fit the name.

After Officer Brooks asked Betsy several more
simple questions, he said, "Why don't you go into the
house and see your mother?"

Betsy took off running.

Kira sent him a silent plea, which he ignored. He
started to follow the child.

"I need to talk to you," she said quietly. He stopped, and
she continued talking. "I'm not comfortable leaving the
little girl here. She was trying to sneak out of her house."

He glanced at the running child, then back to Kira.
"She's not too concerned to go back now."

As soon as she was out of earshot, Kira cleared her
throat and crossed her arms over her chest. "She's afraid
of Mickey, whoever he is."

"Her mother's boyfriend. That's who attacked the
car," Dallas explained. He wrote a few things on his pad
of paper, then put it back into his chest pocket. "We can't
seem to get anyone to admit exactly what happened. The
boy was apparently trying to protect his little sister. I
doubt the guy will be back tonight. Mom seems upset

enough to get a restraining order to keep him out of the house after this." Dallas stopped and faced Kira. "We can't do anything right now. We had Mom perform some maneuvers, and it doesn't appear she's intoxicated. We put out a BOLO for Mickey. Oh, sorry, that means be on the lookout—'"

"I know what a BOLO is. But…" Kira grabbed his arm to keep him from walking away.

He glanced at her hand and pulled his arm from her grip. "I know it isn't easy, Miss Matthews, but it's not a crime to break a window or scold your kids. We don't know that the kid actually hit the man, or whether Mickey hit him first. We simply don't have enough to take further action yet."

She couldn't believe it. "Look, Officer—" She caught herself. "Dallas, I appreciate your attempt to get to the bottom of this, but we are obligated to ensure the children's safety." Kira touched her finger to her chest. "I am, anyway."

"Don't start that battle," Dallas warned. "The boyfriend is gone, and Mom doesn't think he'll be back. For now, that is the best we can ask for. We'll increase patrols in the area. Pete is getting a description as we speak. The boyfriend is probably staying away on purpose, but until he returns, we can't just yank kids away from their custodial parent on a 'maybe' or a hunch."

Kira spoke softly, but firmly. "First of all, I'm not yanking kids away from parents, I'm protecting them.

It isn't a hunch. There's a whole lot more than meets the eye going on here. For one thing, how was a little tiny girl like Betsy able to get out of the basement so easily?"

Dallas shook his head and shrugged his shoulders. "You know as well as I do, kids are industrious. Don't tell me you never snuck out of your parent's house when you were a kid."

She answered without hesitation. "As a matter of fact, I did."

He got a look of satisfaction in his icy blue eyes, without having to say 'I told you so.'

Before he distracted her, Kira added, "I snuck out of every foster home I was in until the Matthews family adopted me. But kids run for a reason. We need to find out why Betsy was sneaking out of her home."

The complacency disappeared from his face. Replaced by a look of dismay. She might have taken some satisfaction in her small victory, but was simply happy to have his attention, finally.

"I'm sorry. I'd have never guessed you had such a difficult childhood." His mouth twisted into a forced smile. "As much as I'd like to change the outcome of this call, Miss Matthews, I can't. No crime has been committed. My gut tells me we don't know the full truth, but we don't have any reason to press charges. If I were a gambler, I would lay odds that we'll be back before the weekend is over. Like you, I hope nothing happens in the meantime."

Kira shook her head. "I'm not waiting to take action. Did you get a good look through the house?"

Dallas shook his head. "Officer Ford hunted for the girl, but he didn't see anything out of line or he'd have said something."

"He obviously didn't check the basement, or he'd have found Betsy. Right?"

Dallas face reddened. "What are you talking about? If you're still upset about me telling you to stay in the car, we followed policy for your protection, and ours."

"I know police policy, Officer. I grew up with it every day. I'm talking about something odd in the basement. Betsy said she locked the secret door."

"What?"

"When I was trying to get Betsy to come out of the basement, I saw an odd glow in the next room. Through a doorway."

Dallas raised an eyebrow. "Glow? Such as?"

"Fluorescent lights. Not the normal glow of table lamps." He wasn't catching her hints. "They have a really large *garden* in the basement."

"I get it, Kira. You think they're growing illegal drugs. I'm trying to stay in chronological order, so, you tried to get her to come out? You instigated it?"

Kira shook her head. "I was standing next to the car, as instructed, when I looked up to see if you were around. Betsy peeked out of the window well and was ready to escape, so I went to talk to her."

Dallas was taking notes. "That's it?"

"No, that's not it. I didn't know if you were coming after her, and if so, if you'd be able to find her if she got out before you caught up with—"

"I'm not questioning your decision, Miss Matthews," he said impatiently. "I'm trying to determine if the suspicious plants were in plain sight or if you went looking for some reason to take the kids away from their mother…."

"Social Services doesn't go looking for reasons to take children from their families." She placed her hands on her hips. "How dare you think such a thing. This is a perfect example of why—"

"Let's stick to this case, if we could." He stared at her with a slight smile as he radioed the other officer. "Officer 138 to PD. Pete, stay with the family."

"I have jurisdiction with the children, you know," Kira said.

Dallas nodded, then took a step toward the house and checked out the basement windows.

"We're not leaving the children here." She felt her blood pressure rise.

"You're barking up the wrong tree, Miss Matthews. I'm on your side. I just want to be sure we do it by the book so the charges stick. Was the window open when you got there to help the girl, or did you open it?" He started walking, shining his flashlight along the foundation. "Let's go back to the window Betsy was in."

"Around the corner, kind of behind that lilac bush, in the shadows…" Kira extended her right arm in that direction as he followed.

"Now, just to clarify, you didn't touch the window at all, and the little girl climbed out on her own?"

"Yes, I knelt down when I got here. I startled her, and she disappeared back into the house. That's when I bent down to look for her. It just looked dark at first, but then I noticed the glow, and a sort of greenhouse in the other room."

Dallas leaned down to peer inside, shining his flashlight in the open window. He turned his light in each direction, and froze. "Whoa," he said with obvious shock.

"What? It's marijuana, right?"

He stood and pulled out his cell phone and dialed immediately. Dallas took several steps away from her and talked so quietly she couldn't hear.

When he returned, he took her by the elbow and led her to the house.

She shook her arm loose. "What's wrong?"

Dallas's mood had turned 180 degrees. "Get the kids ready to get out of here."

"Dallas," Kira said impatiently. "Is it meth?"

He walked closer to her and hurried her along. "Agents from the Drug Enforcement Administration have been watching the guy, Mickey Zelanski, waiting for the chance to bust him and his dealers. We shouldn't have been sent here. They've searched his house half a dozen times and can't find the stash." He motioned to the other officers. "Don't let anyone near that window," he said to them. "The DEA is sending agents over to take over the investigation. Stay out of sight until they arrive." He instructed them where to stand before he returned his attention to Kira. "We need to take care of business as quickly as possible, but first, I need to talk to Betsy, find out how she's getting in there."

"You think that lunatic is watching?"

"With a stash like this, there's no doubt he will be, if he's not already. We need to get out of here."

Kira looked right at him. "A stakeout? Here in Antelope Springs, Colorado?" She fought the urge to glance at the closest neighbor's windows.

"You don't need to know that. Mickey will definitely be back, and when he arrives, he'll have a greeting committee."

Kira still couldn't believe the Drug Enforcement Administration was watching a house here in the middle of rural Colorado. She knew meth labs were common here, but they didn't usually reach the level of the DEA. "Why is the DEA involved?"

"Didn't you notice the bags of meth and bricks of coke in the corner?" he asked quietly.

"Cocaine?" As soon as she said it, she popped her hand over her mouth.

"Who knows what all we're going to find."

Kira looked around. "You're kidding, right?"

"I think you need to get the children out of here as soon as possible."

FIVE

As Kira walked toward the home, she took a deep breath, saying a quick prayer for God to give her wisdom to help this family. She paused before going inside, wondered which foster home, if any, had space available for two kids tonight. "Lord, would you prepare a home for these children while I go through the paperwork? I know the system is full, but I need a miracle, again."

"So, that necklace is more than just a decoration, huh?" Dallas said as he rejoined her again.

"Definitely. I couldn't get through a day without God. Some days we have a lot of talks. What about you?" Kira glanced quickly at the attractive officer, trying not to stare into his touch but tender gaze. *He's nice looking,* she thought.

"We have an on-again off-again relationship, it seems," he said quietly as they reached the door. "In this line of work, you can't survive without God to cover your back, but the attendance records in any church are pretty dismal."

"That's the nature of the job, unfortunately." Kira didn't have time to think about his comments now. She had work to do. While the drug task force evaluated the contamination threat of the home, Kira and Dallas convinced the mother that she had no options left. Finally, Shirley gave the information Kira needed about parents and possible extended family members who might be able to take care of the children while she was "away." Kira explained that a family group conference would be scheduled to meet with a review committee from Social Services to discuss care of the children. In the meantime, Kira would investigate the suitability of each family member.

The mother was angry, Cody quiet and Betsy just plain afraid. A female officer came and sat with the kids in the other room while Kira talked with the mother.

"Agents from the Drug Enforcement Administration will be here soon," Dallas said, prompting her to finish up. "They'd like the kids out of here before they arrive. We need to have a doctor make sure the kids haven't been exposed to any harmful chemicals or drugs."

The mother began swearing again as they were taken away.

"What about the drugs," Kira asked quietly. "Are they making them in the home, too?"

"No, it's not a kitchen, so we don't have those risks to deal with. But just in case, they've had the children change clothes. And since it's become such a big problem in the area, we have those new regulations to follow. We need to have the children checked out at the hospital. As for Mickey and Shirley, their problems are much bigger than you can imagine. Best we just get the kids into a home, where they can move on."

Her jaw dropped.

"Come on, how soon will you be ready?" Dallas motioned toward the kids' bedrooms. "Let's get their things and go, so that the DEA can do their work."

Kira looked around each child's room. There wasn't much that they would be allowed to take, yet somehow they'd filled a few bags. "Anything else you need?"

"I want my bear!" Betsy demanded.

Dallas knelt down next to the girl. "I have a brand-new stuffed animal I'd like to give you, Betsy. I know it's not the same but—"

"I want *my* bear."

Kira offered Betsy a hug, while Cody hit them all over the head with the cold, hard facts. "They had to take it, Betsy. Mickey stuffed it with drugs, remember? The police have to take it now." His voice was filled with bitterness.

"Mama…" Betsy whimpered.

It never failed to amaze Kira that children clung to the familiar even when it wasn't worth holding on to. Getting the kids' essentials together drained her, for it brought back too many memories of her own childhood misery.

"We need to leave now," she said softly. "I'm going

to find a nice home for you to stay at until I've had a chance to talk with your aunt."

"No, I want Mommy," Betsy whined, running down the hallway.

Dallas caught her and lifted her into his arms. "Come on, Betsy, let's find that new toy I have for you." He carried her to the patrol car while Cody lagged defiantly behind.

What little rapport Kira had managed to build with the girl diminished just as quickly once Betsy figured out she was being taken away from her mother. She wanted nothing to do with Kira now.

Cody caught up with Officer Brooks immediately when Betsy screamed for her mother.

"I'll take care of her, she's my sister." Cody puffed his scrawny chest out and reached for Betsy. Officer Brooks relinquished the little girl without a word.

That surprised her, but why, Kira wasn't sure. She studied him a moment before turning to watch the boy's response to his sister's fear.

"It's going to be okay, Bets," Cody said in a soothing voice. "I promise, I'll take care of you." He paused only long enough for Dallas to open the back door of Officer Williams's patrol car. Williams had taken Dallas's cruiser to the impound lot for the investigator to run prints and record the damage. They didn't want the kids to see the destruction Mickey had done. They'd already been through enough.

As Cody waited for his sister to climb into the car, he turned to Officer Brooks. "Thanks, man," he said quietly.

Kira couldn't believe what she thought she heard. She shot a quick glance at Dallas just in time to see him deliberately wipe a smile from his face. "Just doing my job."

Kira carried the children's belongings, feeling slightly left out. She couldn't remember the last time anyone had thanked her for removing them from a dangerous home setting. She waited for Dallas to close the door before she said anything. "What was *that* about?"

"It's our job. You can't let feelings get in the way."

She stood there, stunned, while Dallas took the grocery bags holding the kids' few belongings, and put them into the trunk. She knew he was right, but it didn't stop the pain. She was the one who'd been terrorized, she'd found Betsy, then she'd convinced Dallas that they needed to be removed from the home. Yet he received the thanks, the hugs and the glory.

How dare he claim they couldn't let themselves get emotionally involved? "How, exactly, do you turn off the emotions, Officer Brooks?"

"I thought we agreed that you'd call me Dallas. I'm doing my job. There's no room for emotions."

She didn't believe him for a minute. "Job well done, then. If you wouldn't mind taking us to the police station so I can get my car, I'd appreciate it."

"I'll be happy to, after we have the kids checked out

at the hospital. Hopefully, that won't take too long, since the house wasn't where the meth was cooked."

Kira called the Social Services number and discussed the case with the staff member on duty. A few minutes later, as Dallas and Kira waited for clearance from the hospital, she said, "The intake caseworker is having trouble finding a home where we can keep the children together. As usual, we're overloaded with children, and understaffed with foster homes."

While she was talking, Dallas dug through a box in the trunk filled with stuffed toys. Finally he pulled out a golden bunny. "Think she'll like this?"

"It might distract her for now." Kira knew it was unlikely that a new stuffed animal would console Betsy for the loss of Fuzzy Bear, but it was worth a try. What Betsy wanted was security, and right now, that felt a long way off to a little girl.

Dallas tossed the golden-yellow bunny into the air and caught it with his other hand. "It's going to be a long road for these kids, isn't it?"

"I'm afraid so," Kira agreed.

"Here." He handed the toy to Kira. "You give it to her."

She caught it, startled by the unexpected gesture. The softness of the fur surprised her as well. When she looked up to thank Dallas, he was already in the car.

After a slight hesitation, she opened the back door and climbed inside. "Dal…" She caught herself. "Officer Brooks found this for you, Betsy. We know it won't be the same as Fuzzy." She paused to brush the soft fur one more time. "But if you close your eyes and snuggle her, it feels soft and fuzzy like your bear." Kira handed the toy to Betsy. "Look, the bunny's fur is the same color as your hair."

Betsy closed her eyes and brushed the bunny against her cheek. A tiny smile replaced the pout. "Thank you." She hugged the animal and held it up for her brother's approval, and it even brought a brief smile to his face.

Two hours later, both kids had a clean bill of health and Kira was on her way to the short-term foster care home. It would be a couple of days before Social Services could evaluate the aunt's qualifications as a kinship provider. Unfortunately, the only place in the county that had room for both children on short notice was thirty minutes away. Since the intake caseworker who was on call lived in the opposite direction from the foster home, Kira had agreed to drop the kids off on her way home. "Are you two hungry? I can stop and get you a hamburger."

"That would be good, thanks," Cody said quietly.

Kira turned into the only fast-food restaurant in town with a drive-up window. If the kids had a full stomach, they would be more content, the drive would go quicker, plus they would have something to keep them busy. They had enough to think about right now without hunger being one of them.

The children gave her their order and Kira pulled forward to wait for the food.

"I want Mommy," Betsy whimpered.

Kira glanced into the rearview mirror at the little girl, who kept a tight grip on her brother with one skinny little arm.

"Mom's sick, Betsy. She needs to go to the doctor and get help," the teen said.

The words of wisdom startled Kira, even while she knew the anger he expressed earlier wasn't gone. It couldn't be. According to their files, Cody had to know what was coming. They'd been through this before. Betsy probably didn't remember going through it the last time. She had been just a year and a half old.

Kira had read their file while the intake caseworker had finished up the paperwork. How could their mother have come so far and then let herself slip up again?

SIX

Dallas typed out the report and sent it to the shift supervisor's electronic queue so he could move on with his evening. His thoughts sped back to Kira and how she wore her heart on her sleeve. He admired that, even though he knew it would one day backfire on her.

He kept the radio on, hoping to hear that Mickey had been apprehended. No such luck. If Mickey Zelanski was easy to locate and apprehend, he wouldn't be on the Most Wanted list.

As the image of the doper replayed in his mind, Dallas shook his head, wishing there was something he could do to make the evening's events disappear. He despised it when innocent bystanders became victims, especially when drugs were involved.

"How're you doing?" the shift supervisor asked from the doorway.

Dallas flinched at the sudden voice over his shoulder. He hoped Sergeant Shaline didn't overreact to his edginess. He'd have had the same reaction any night. Tonight was nothing out of the ordinary. "I'm done with the paperwork and ready to get back on patrol." He glanced over his shoulder.

"Stop in my office for a minute before you do."

"Aw, come on, I'm on top of it." *It* being watching for any signs of post-traumatic stress disorder.

Shaline nodded. "Good. We'll talk about it in a few minutes."

Dallas closed his eyes and took a deep breath. *I'm fine,* he thought silently. He, of all people, didn't want to lose another three years of his life to PTSD. He wouldn't let himself. It was out of the question.

Dallas headed over to the sergeant's office. "So you want to know how I'm feeling," Dallas said sarcastically, waiting impatiently to be released.

"No, I want to know *what* you're feeling."

Dallas didn't respond, as he was still thinking about the answer.

"Humor me, Brooks. Just talk it through for a few minutes. I wouldn't be doing my job if I didn't speak with you about this. And you wouldn't have been hired at all if we didn't think you were ready to be back on the job. We just need to make sure we don't stick our heads in the sand and pretend it never happened."

Dallas grumbled. "If you want to become a psychologist, Shaline, go back to school. Besides, you don't even have a couch to lie on."

Shaline leveled him a look and Dallas dropped into the chair. "I'm angry that I was caught off guard," he admitted, after thinking a minute. "I'm angry that an innocent woman was caught in the middle." Kira again flashed into his thoughts and he shoved them away. "And I want to get back out there and do my job. I'm not going home."

"I wouldn't let you if you wanted to. It wasn't your fault. Miss Matthews is also trained to go into homes, most often without backup." Shaline stood up and closed the door. "None of us would have been expecting this."

"You've talked to her?" Dallas said, cringing.

"No, should I?"

He shook his head. "It's just that she made the same point, about social workers." Her spunk scared him. She didn't seem to realize that even good intentions could end in disaster.

"I hear she made a call on the radio. What did you think when you heard that?"

Dallas felt his jaw tense. "I didn't think it was her. It didn't sound like her. I was talking to an uncooperative mother and her son…." No one could absolve him from his guilt. "I didn't hear anything going on outside, but I should have listened instead of ignoring the frantic tone of her voice. I figured it was the dispatcher's job to radio an official response. I didn't turn my radio down all the way."

The sergeant was quiet.

"If we're done here…" Dallas stood to leave.

"Not so quick," he admonished. He issued the required reprimand, followed by another reminder that he himself would likely have reacted the same way. "And while we're talking about Miss Matthews…"

"Were we?"

"Did the topic of officer response time come up?"

"What? Why would that come up?" When Shaline waited, Dallas told him, "No, it never came up. Practically as soon as I got into the car I got the call for a hang-up."

"She was here to observe officer response time to Child Protection Services calls." He had a way of talking with his hands, and made an all-encompassing gesture. "This problem isn't about you, or tonight."

Dallas jumped to his feet. "Thanks for the heads-up," he said indignantly.

"She showed up unannounced and requested the officer not know ahead of time." The sergeant motioned to the chair and waited for Dallas to sit down again. "There have been several complaints over the last few years about law enforcement officers' response time when backup is requested by caseworkers. She's talking with all law enforcement agencies in the county. Tonight you showed that slow response time isn't the norm in our department. Thank you for that."

Air hissed through Dallas's teeth.

Shaline continued. "What happened didn't likely help her overall opinion, but I think we're okay. You didn't do anything wrong, Dallas. It's a learning experience for all of us."

"Did the DEA know there were kids in the house?"

Shaline shook his head, shrugging his shoulders at the same time. "I don't know. None of it should have gone this far. There's some confusion about Mickey's address. The kids are safe now, and hopefully, soon, DEA will have another supplier in custody. In the meantime, I'd like you to stop by Miss Matthews's place and see how she's doing."

Dallas couldn't believe it. "Tonight?"

"Don't let her walk away scared, Brooks. When you fall off a horse, get back on and ride it. You ought to know that better than any other officer on the force."

Dallas swallowed hard. "Excuse me, sir, but it took me three years to work through it and get back on that horse."

"But you did," Shaline said. He went into the story about his daughter's first car accident. "The hardest thing I ever did as a parent was to pick Sami up at the scene and put her right back behind the wheel to drive us both home. But she needed to know I had confidence in her."

Dallas silently wondered what any of this had to do with what had happened tonight. "And I'm sure it made her a better driver in the long run, right?"

"It did. It was the worst ride-along I've ever done, but I'd do it again in a heartbeat."

"You'd do anything for Sami." Dallas looked at his

watch. "Miss Matthews could misunderstand if I show up in the middle of the night."

Shaline laughed. "So call her first. I don't think she'll mistake your concern. You're a professional following up on a bad situation. She's an excellent addition to Child Protection. We can't afford to lose her. See if she'd like to finish the ride-along." He handed Dallas a slip of paper. "Here's her address, and the phone number she listed on her release form. And take car number 38. I've made arrangements for investigations to dust for fingerprints and look for any other evidence on your cruiser before they send it in for repairs."

Dallas took the paper and went directly to another patrol car, driving an hour before coming to terms with what he had to do. There was no way he was going into Fossil Creek looking for her address at midnight. Dallas drove around the block, then pulled into the grocery store parking lot on Main Street. He took out his cell phone.

The phone rang four times, then went to voice mail. "Hello, this is Kira Matthews with Poudre County Child Protection Services. If this is an emergency, please dial 911. If it is in reference to an urgent child protection case, please press number 4 and you will be directed to the twenty-four-hour help line. Otherwise, please leave your name and number. I will return your call the next business day." The woman didn't leave anything out.

Dallas smiled, ignoring his annoyance with being

told to follow up on her. He wanted to think he'd have done it himself at a more suitable hour.

He heard the beep and automatically left a message. "Hi, this is Dallas Brooks—" he was feeling a little punchy this time of night and decided maybe Kira could use a laugh, too "—with Antelope Springs Police Department. I believe we met at a crime scene this evening. I'm calling to make sure that you're okay and to see if you're interested in finishing the ride-along…sometime. I'll also need you to come into the station and fill out a report. My cell phone number is 555-4357." He ended the call and put the phone in the clip on his belt.

When he began his patrol again, a shadow of Kira kept him company. They had been together only a few minutes, he realized, once he considered the time he'd been inside the house. So why was he still thinking about her? Maybe it was the nagging realization that he had no business going by Miss Matthews's house at any hour. As if that wasn't enough to eat at his conscience. He dragged in a deep breath, wishing he was the kind of guy who could keep it casual with women. He wasn't, and never had been. Therefore, he had to get her big brown eyes out of his mind. He had already caused her enough pain.

He figured he'd get a call back on Monday, but an hour later, his phone rang. He didn't recognize the number. "Dallas Brooks," he answered.

"Dallas, this is Kira. I just got your message."

"You're back at the office? Or are you *still* at the office?"

"Oh no, I'm home. I'm just trying to wind down. There are a million and one questions going through my head." She sounded tired and vulnerable. To be expected after what she'd been through. "How do you turn it all off when you get home?"

Dallas pulled off the street into a parking lot and stopped. Was he really willing to open Pandora's box? How could he tell her that there were nights, still, when the visions never completely went away? "Most nights are so quiet after a big call that the boredom gives me plenty of time to unwind." Dallas kept his eye on traffic while he talked. "Sergeant Shaline wanted me to check on you and see if you want to finish your ride-along tonight."

"I'm doing fine, Officer Brooks." Her voice had that business tone to it again. "Overprocessing is normal for me, but no, I don't want to go back out tonight. I was riding along to discuss my own agenda, and I have to admit, that's not on the top of my list now."

Dallas could sympathize with her. "Yeah, I didn't suppose you would, but I thought I'd ask." The take-charge person wanted to compartmentalize her life. Put everything in its place. He knew what she was going through. It wasn't easy to pigeonhole this kind of incident.

"So you can report back that I'm doing just fine."

Ah, so she didn't mind when it was him asking, but if he'd been told to, she didn't want to talk. He had been wrong to bring up the sergeant's name, apparently. "How did the kids take to the foster home?"

"Fine," she said abruptly. "I'm fine, they're fine, we'll *all* be fine. That's what you want, right?"

She was part shrink, too, apparently. He took a deep breath, remembering his own anger at being told to talk it out. She was right; he did want everything to be "fine." Unfortunately, this was the real world he was working in again, where dysfunction was the norm. If it wasn't, he likely wouldn't have a job. "Kira, I'm sorry. I wish none of this had happened, and that I could have prevented you from experiencing such an ugly side of society."

She didn't speak, but he could hear her breathing. Was she crying? Or trying to stuff the emotions away? He wished he was with her now.

"I don't blame you for being angry. It shouldn't have happened," he added. "I know how upsetting it is."

"You don't have to console me," she insisted. "I'm not upset."

"I understand," he said. He wasn't going to argue. "If you do decide you need someone to listen, I'm here."

"Dallas, have they caught him yet?"

"Not that I've heard, but the Drug Enforcement Administration agents have taken over. They're working with the Drug Task Force officers on it, so I probably won't hear much now."

"That's a lousy excuse."

"It's a lousy situation, but that's the way the system

works. They have a case to build, and this incident threw a kink into their surveillance. We have to let them deal with it now."

Their call was interrupted twice when dispatch called to check his status. Yet Dallas noticed that Kira never actually made a move to get off the phone.

"The DEA works pretty quietly, at least as far as not involving the street cops. We'll probably not have too much to do with it unless Mickey gets stopped for a traffic violation. That happens quite a bit, in fact." He explained a few cases where drug dealers had gone to prison for charges totally unrelated to their drug involvement.

Finally, Kira agreed to ride along again in the near future. "Will that convince you and Sergeant Shaline that I'm not abandoning my mission to get our agencies to work out our problems?"

"I don't know about the sergeant, but it makes me feel a little better, even though I don't know anything about why you really came tonight." Dallas didn't know much about her mission, but it seemed like a good idea to keep it on the back burner right now. After what had happened tonight, it wouldn't take much to boil over into an ugly situation. "However, I don't think I can wait a week to see you."

Kira was silent, and Dallas wondered if she'd hung up on him. "Kira?"

"You...can't?" she said in a whisper. Her voice had an odd note to it suddenly.

Was she okay? "No, not really," he said cautiously, trying to read between the lines. "I know the evening didn't exactly go as you had planned. We hardly got a chance to talk."

"We're talking now."

"You know what I mean."

"So what is it you want to talk about?" she asked in a lighter tone.

"You were the one who came to talk about something. I'm curious to hear more about your project."

"Oh," she said, obviously taken aback. "Is that what you meant by you couldn't wait a full week to see me?"

"No, that was in reference to filling out a report on what happened tonight."

"You certainly know how to take the wind out of a girl's sails, Officer Brooks." Now she sounded almost angry. What had he done?

"Dallas," he said, realizing too late that she had been flirting with him. Much as he'd like to investigate the possibility of a personal relationship, that was out of the question. He stammered over his words. "Miss Matthews… Kira… I didn't—"

"Obviously not. I don't know what—" She coughed. "I don't know what I was thinking," she stammered in turn. "Yeah, it's been a long night."

"Exactly." Dallas wasn't sure how this whole conversation had gotten so misconstrued, and why it disappointed him. "Consider yourself fortunate. The sergeant doesn't usually let anyone leave without filling out the paperwork."

"Not to worry," she said in a chastising voice. "I always take care of the paperwork. I'll get it to you. Stay safe."

The line went silent, and he didn't think it was accidental. Dallas paused a few minutes to consider whether or not he should phone her back. The call had ended abruptly. Then again, she knew how to reach him if she needed to. And he didn't have one doubt that she would never need to.

He pulled his police car out to the street to finish the last couple of hours of his shift. Even the mundane traffic stops couldn't keep his mind off Kira and the unexpected turn in their conversation. He didn't know how she'd gotten the impression that he was flirting with her. There was no way…. None whatsoever.

Three years, five months and fifteen days ago, Dallas had turned in his badge and walked away from police work, parched as the Arizona desert. It had been pointless to stay in Phoenix after he and his fiancée had ended their relationship. Odds of a successful marriage were lethal enough in law enforcement alone, but mixed with the diagnosis of post-traumatic stress disorder, they were abysmal. There was no way, after all that, that he'd have given Miss Matthews the impression that he was interested in her.

He and God had argued long and hard before Dallas returned to law enforcement. He had drifted from one job to another, moving from Arizona through New Mexico and finally to Colorado, before he realized he couldn't run far or fast enough to get the desire to protect and serve out of his blood. He hadn't chosen his career, it had chosen him. Letting go of his dreams of a marriage and family were far easier than turning away from God's plan.

So why was it so difficult to keep Kira Matthews from invading his every thought?

SEVEN

Later that week, Kira listened to Dallas's voice mails, then deleted them. She'd taken a few days off work, blaming the migraine that had hit in the middle of the night. She wasn't sure if the headache was the root of her problems, or if the root of her problems caused the migraine. No matter which was the case, she'd hurt from her head to her toes.

She had tried to drive to Antelope Springs Police Department three times since the incident, and she just couldn't do it. How could thirty miles seem as difficult as crossing the Grand Canyon?

She'd felt like an idiot, flirting with Dallas, when he had not been doing the same. She just couldn't bring herself to face him or answer his calls. She had phoned the precinct to ask if she could fax a statement to them, but that wasn't allowed. They felt the officer filing the report would want to ask her a few questions. Great.

She had considered asking one of her brothers for

his help, but then she'd have to tell him why. She couldn't do that. She couldn't embarrass her family by telling them she'd lost her composure on a ride-along. They were all brave police officers who would never let her live it down if they found out their little sister was such a chicken.

She knew that until the statement was out of the way, she wasn't going to be able to put it behind her. And she desperately needed to do just that.

Her peaceful sleep was interrupted by recurring nightmares of the incident. Each scene played out in full, over and over. She couldn't seem to stop the wheels turning, wondering what might've happened if she'd gone into the house alone. If Dallas hadn't been there…

Dallas, who apparently wasn't flirting with her.

Dallas, with the massive shoulders, compelling blue eyes and well-hidden compassion. Her face flushed at the memory of his rejection, and she brushed the thought away when the traffic light turned green. Dallas was a red light, unavoidable, but good at testing her patience. She just didn't understand how she could have been so wrong about him.

Kira's instincts had served her well up until now. But if she couldn't stop doubting herself, it wouldn't be long before her job suffered. She had to find a way to get through this, and soon. Since the incident, she'd been on call only one night. She had prayed all day for a quiet evening and was blessed with answered prayers.

She only had a few more nights' reprieve. Hopefully, that would give her enough time to get over it.

As she pulled into the parking lot of her condominium, she anxiously looked around for anyone lurking nearby. Kira turned into her garage, a feature she'd agreed to in order to keep her brothers from pestering her about security. She waited until the garage door was all the way to the ground before getting out of the car.

She'd never been so thankful for the added security of the private entry than she had been since the police car she'd been sitting in was attacked right outside someone's home. She'd gone into situations like that at night dozens of times. She couldn't let her head keep playing tug-of-war with her emotions like this.

By the time she unloaded her groceries and locked herself inside her condo, she was mentally exhausted. Kira dropped the mail on the table, noticing the envelope from Family Finders. That meant they hadn't found her brother yet. She ripped it open and unfolded the latest computer generated report. It had jumped from two pages to five. She felt her heart race as she read through the new information. "Jimmie Driscoe— arrested for domestic disturbance, charges dropped; employment verification—Livingston Motors, four months, fired, failed drug test; arrested for possession of drugs, in drug rehab—" and the list went on.

She flipped to the last page to verify that they hadn't made contact with him yet, then tossed the report into her mail basket on the table. She closed her eyes and recited one of her favorite Bible verses: "'When you pass through deep waters I will be with you. Your troubles will not overwhelm you…. Will not overwhelm you.'" She repeated, and took a deep breath.

"God help me get some sleep tonight," she whispered as she started the microwave to heat her dinner. "I feel like that guy is out there, waiting to seek revenge against me for shutting down his business." She thought back to the interview with Betsy earlier this morning. It still made Kira angry. How could a mother chop and bag cocaine for sale, then turn and feed her daughter bread sliced on the same cutting board? The kids had also been with their mom on numerous occasions when she'd distributed the drugs.

Shirley had sobbed throughout the family group meeting when she realized she wouldn't get her children back. This was her third drug arrest. And this time she was going to be in prison for a long time on trafficking charges. None of the family had proved to be suitable guardians, and Kira was forced, earlier than usual, to discuss giving the children up for adoption as Shirley's best option. Kira wondered if the woman would ever get control over her drug problems.

She filled a glass of water and set it next to her chair by the gas fireplace. She was getting ready to grab her dinner from the microwave when a knock on the door scared her out of her skin. She gave a small yelp, right before whoever it was knocked a second time. Kira ran to her purse and grabbed her Mace, then looked through the peephole, to find her mother standing there. Kira felt relief wash through her.

"Hi," she said as she opened the door. Suddenly, she remembered the Mace, hid it behind her and backed away from the door, hoping to find somewhere to put it before her mother saw it.

Her mom looked at Kira, seeming to know immediately that something was wrong. "Hi," she said, with a cautious glance around the condo. "So, what's wrong?"

Saying "nothing" would be too obvious. Kira wanted to deny the accusation, but knew it was useless. "Bad week, why?" She walked past the kitchen, sliding the Mace around her body to keep it out of sight.

Her mom followed her into the cluttered living room, where Kira sat down and stuffed the container under the chair cushion. "Yesterday was Garrett's birthday. You didn't show up for dinner. Tonight was the concert at church, and you were going to meet us there. Are you okay?"

Brushing the hair from her face, Kira felt a stab of guilt. "I wasn't feeling well, but I can't believe I forgot…" She and Garrett were only months apart in age, which had created a bit of tension when they were kids. He'd been the baby until they had adopted her, just a week before his birthday. A little sister wasn't exactly on the top of his birthday wish list, then or now. Not only had he gotten a sister, she'd bumped him out of his baby of the family role. It took earning her master's degree to figure out why his reaction to that really wasn't anything he could have controlled. "Is Garrett upset with me?"

Her mother hesitated, obviously caught off guard by Kira's direct question. "Well, he didn't say so…."

Kira finished the sentence. "But he thinks it was intentional. It wasn't. I had a bad experience the other night on a call, and I'm not dealing with it very well." She hoped that was enough to keep her mom from asking any questions. "I'll call him and explain."

The concern on her mother's face deepened. "What happened? Why didn't you phone and tell us?"

Kira hesitated. She didn't need to worry her parents, and if her dad heard about what had happened, he'd become her constant bodyguard. That wouldn't help. She should have been prepared, and that bothered her. "I responded to a call, and the boyfriend showed up and got upset."

"He didn't hurt you, did he?" her mom said as she pushed the ottoman closer.

Kira shook her head.

"I wish you'd have chosen any profession but social work. It's so dangerous for you to go into homes alone…." her mom said as she sat down.

Kira felt the temptation to let herself relax and tell her mom everything. "I wasn't alone," she said, unable to go on. She was about to cry. But she didn't want her family to know how foolish she'd been. "The police were there, too. I'm fine. A little wobbly, but I'm going to be okay. I'm just tired."

Kira had spent a lot of time lately thinking about the struggles she'd gone through when Ted and Grace Matthews adopted her. She hadn't wanted their comfort. Hadn't trusted them. It had taken months for her to believe this family was hers for good. She didn't want three bossy big brothers. She wanted her own little brother. And in those days, the Matthews trio sure didn't act like they wanted a little sister. She'd even thought it was their fault that her brother, Jimmie, had been taken away from her. For years she'd blamed them. In her five-year-old mind, they didn't want a sister, but they didn't *need* another brother. They already had three boys; why would they want a fourth?

"Why didn't you call us? That's what family is for, Kira." Mom brushed the unruly curls from Kira's face.

She simply shrugged, not trusting herself to speak. Why, after all these years, was she still afraid of doing something wrong and being sent away? It was ridiculous. She wasn't a five-year-old anymore.

She glanced over to the letter from Family Finders. It had been years since she'd first told her mother that she wanted to find Jimmie. Though Grace claimed to understand, she couldn't hide her disappointment. Kira tried to reassure her mother that it had nothing to do with her love for her family. She had always felt guilty that she had let Jimmie down.

Kira pulled her legs to her chest and wrapped her arms around them, her mind drifting back to Betsy and Cody and what they were likely feeling tonight.

Her mom watched silently, then perked up. "It's been a long time since you've slept over at home. Maybe this would be a good time. Let us pamper you for a few days. Catch up on your sleep, enjoy that new jetted tub your dad put in for me. It just melts those aches away," she cooed, as if the tub were filled with chocolate.

A chuckle escaped, and Kira felt the idea taking hold. *After a few days of sleep, I'll be back to myself,* she thought. Her mom always seemed to know when Kira needed a safety net to fall into. She didn't want to slink back home, but it felt like this might be just what she needed. Even though her parents lived less than five miles away, there was nothing quite as comforting as being home.

Kira nodded. "Maybe it would." It would be a lot more challenging to keep the truth quiet there, but she wasn't sleeping at all here. Every noise startled her awake. Knowing that her dad would be there to ward off Mickey, should he appear, would be a huge comfort. If that didn't allow her to rest, nothing would.

"Why don't we pack a bag now?" Mom glanced around the apartment, forcing Kira to realize it was getting more and more difficult to think of anything but the incident. Her laundry was tossed over the furniture, dishes were piled in the sink and even the groceries she'd just bought were on the counters instead of in the cupboard. She'd been a neat freak all her life, keeping all of her belongings in one place, just in case.... It wasn't any surprise that her mom was concerned.

"You can stay as long as you want," Mom told her.

"Maybe a day or two?" Kira's mind wandered to the hot tub, the pillow-top bed, and her daddy to protect her. "If you're sure it's okay…"

Mom let out a gasp of exasperation. "Kira Danae! You're always welcome. You don't need an invitation."

"Okay, okay. I'll go." Her birth mom couldn't have understood her any better than her adopted mother, Kira silently admitted. "I'll go pack a bag." She grabbed her mail basket and rushed up the stairs before her mom noticed anything.

Kira knew her doubts were foolish, but she couldn't seem to control any of her emotions this week. Though she hadn't gone to the office, she'd talked to Cody and Betsy's foster mom twice since they'd moved in. It wasn't going well at all. Tomorrow she needed to meet with them again.

Mom had always said that she and Kira were more alike than blood could provide. God had blessed Kira so much when he'd delivered her, six years late maybe, to the Matthewses' home. And despite the sometimes strained feelings with her brothers through the years, she knew they loved her as much as they could have any sister.

But sometimes she needed to remind herself that sibling struggles had nothing to do with her being adopted and not being wanted. The adoption had no more to do with their relationship than their different race or skin color. They were as close and irritating as blood relatives, so why was it still instinctive to worry that if she made them mad, they'd send her away?

"Thanks, God. You always seem to know when I need my family most."

EIGHT

"You're going to have to get the social worker back in here, Brooks. I need her statement," Sergeant Shaline said, stepping out of his office. He dropped the report on the bench next to Dallas.

It had been a week since the incident, and Dallas still hadn't heard from Kira Matthews. But it wasn't for a lack of trying. "I've phoned every shift. She doesn't return my calls."

"Doesn't sound good. Before you head out, you need to see the captain."

"Now?"

"If you're going on patrol, then yes, before you head out would be now."

There has to be a wise guy in every crowd. Dallas walked up the stairs of the station and knocked on the officer's open door. "Hi, Captain. Sergeant Shaline said you—"

"Sit down, Dallas." Captain Galyard straightened a

stack of papers by tapping the full bundle on the desk, then moved it out of the way. Finally, he turned his attention to Dallas. "I need to reassign you for a few weeks."

"Okay," Dallas said with interest. "Which shift?"

The captain stalled a few more minutes, staring at him. "Days." He paused, as if that was supposed to upset Dallas.

What's all the drama about? "Not a problem," he said aloud, even though he wasn't thrilled. Days were nice for the schedule, as long as you liked traffic and cold calls. "When do I start?"

"Tomorrow," Captain Galyard said. "Report to the high school. The school resource officer—"

Dallas's reaction was instantaneous, and he knew the captain was expecting it. He took a deep breath. "You're joking, right?" He thought a second. Was it April Fool's Day, or just another of the captain's practical jokes? This was no joking matter. Not even Galyard, king of pranksters, would put him through this. Would he?

"I'm afraid not, Dallas. Brad Johnson needs some time off. He'll go over the school policies with you tomorrow—"

"Wait just a minute." Dallas shook his head. This was the last thing he'd expected to hear. "Back up. You're serious?"

Captain Galyard gave him a look that dared him to question an order. "I wouldn't joke with you about this,

Dallas. Brad's going on medical leave, and it can't wait. I know this is going to be tough for you, but we don't have time to train a new school resource officer, and no one else in the precinct has any experience."

Dallas felt his world turn upside down. The flashback to his last day as an SRO was quick, but no doubt complete. The actual event hadn't taken much longer. With one gunshot, Steve Waverley's baseball hopes were gone, and Alek Beeson was dead.

This wasn't in the deal, God. I agreed to come back to protect and serve. I said no kids. No schools. We had an agreement.

What was he thinking, arguing with God? He'd already tried that, and God had led him to Antelope Springs, a quiet rural town in northern Colorado. What could happen here? He shook his head.

"You're trained, you have invaluable experience and we need you there, Dallas…."

Though his head was nodding, Dallas wasn't really absorbing any of the conversation. After a few minutes, he pulled himself out of his fog. "Does anyone else know what happened in Phoenix?"

"It's nobody's business but ours. There is nothing in your personnel file on it, if that's your concern. It's just for a few weeks, then school will be out for the summer. Hopefully, Johnson will be back on the job in the fall. I'm here anytime you need to talk. Anytime, night or day, and I expect to hear from you."

A few weeks. Surely I can hang on for a few weeks. "I'll make it work." He stood to leave.

"Unless it's unusually busy tonight, leave as soon as you get Miss Matthews's statement. School starts at 7:25 a.m., so Johnson would like to meet with you at 6:30 a.m."

"Yes, sir," he muttered. At least the captain didn't expect him to work a double shift.

He called Kira from the station, hoping he could make it a quick deal, get her over here to write up her statement so he could finish the report and be done with it. No such luck. He stopped into Sergeant Shaline's office again and let him know he wasn't able to reach her.

"I guess you're driving to Fossil Creek, then, aren't you? If that doesn't produce any results, you might consider putting out a BOLO for her," he chuckled.

"Yeah, that ought to build a few bridges between us and Social Services, wouldn't it?" Dallas replied, shaking his head. The last thing he wanted tonight was to chase the woman down. He had made every attempt to get her here already.

Thirty minutes later he was surprised to find a security gate at the entrance to her upscale village of Victorian style town homes. *Looks like they pay social workers a lot more than they do cops these days.* He parked in the visitors lot, wound his way on foot through the streets to her condo and rang the bell. No answer. *Why am I not surprised?*

He pulled out her release form from her ride-along

and dialed the number listed for next of kin, only to get the Office of Protective Services, again. This time, though, he followed the instructions to reach an after-hours operator. After he'd explained the situation, the woman put him on hold for what seemed like forever.

"Officer Brooks," the operator finally announced, "Miss Matthews hasn't been at work for the last three days."

"She's sick?"

"Don't know. I just know she's been out."

"Thanks. Do you have an emergency contact for her?"

"You'd have to call her supervisor tomorrow for that."

"Yeah. Thanks." Dallas knew it was ridiculous to believe the worst, but he couldn't take that chance. The DEA hadn't arrested Mickey Zelanski yet. What if, for some idiotic reason, he'd come after Kira?

She hadn't returned his calls, and he couldn't even get hold of her at work. He'd come this far, and he wasn't giving up now. He didn't want to make another mistake. Not with Kira.

He rang the doorbell again, and not expecting a different response, looked for an open curtain so he could peek inside. He froze when he saw a window gaping wide. He shone his flashlight around the yard, looking for other signs of an intruder, then back into the house.

"Kira?" He shone the light along the wall, able to make a guess as to the layout of the unit. It looked like she had a living room and kitchen on the main floor, bedrooms upstairs. He took a step, and his foot caught on something. Dallas looked down and saw the screen to the window. Immediately, he pulled out his cell phone and called the local police department to send an officer.

While he waited, he looked around the yard for anything else that was out of place. When an officer arrived, he was so young he looked like he should be reading Shakespeare in high school English class. "Officer Richards." He extended his hand, "You must be Officer Brooks?"

Dallas nodded, then explained the situation in full.

"Matthews? We have an officer on the force by that name. What's she look like?"

Dallas didn't have to think about that, "African American, light brown skin, brown hair, brown eyes, slim…" While Dallas described her, the officer took notes.

The kid shook his newly buzzed head. "Must not be related. So the place looks like it's been broken into…." He jotted more notes, then looked up again. "When did you talk to her last?"

"It's been almost a week, and apparently her office hasn't seen her for several days, either."

"Have you talked to any of the neighbors, asked if they've seen her?"

"Not yet," Dallas said, wishing he could speed things along. He began to pace, anxious to make sure he hadn't left another innocent victim in the path of destruction. While the obviously new cop asked the standard questions about a missing person, going back and forth on the cell phone with his supervisor, Dallas knocked on doors. He was perplexed that no one had seen or heard anything out of the ordinary, and no one had set eyes on her in several days.

When he returned, the kid was on with dispatch. "Be on the lookout for Kira Matthews, a social worker with Poudre County, about thirty years old, light brown skin, brown hair and brown eyes, five foot seven. Last seen in Antelope Springs, Colorado, on Friday evening. Need to do a welfare check at her home."

"Hold on, Officer Richards," the dispatcher said.

Over the radio they heard another officer respond that he would be right there. Within minutes, a detective showed up in plain clothes, wearing his badge on his belt and a phone to his ear. With him was a corporal in a regular patrol uniform.

Dallas could hear the phone ringing inside the unit again. "Come on, Kira, answer," the detective muttered. He looked at Dallas and nodded. "I'm Nick Matthews and this is Garrett."

"Dallas Brooks, from Antelope Springs Police Department."

"You're the one looking for Kira?" the corporal asked as he opened the storm door and pulled a key from his pocket.

"Yeah, I need her to complete some paperwork."

"Um, did either of you try to bust in?" The corporal

turned toward them. "Get your camera, Nick. The door wasn't like this last time I saw Kira."

"We didn't touch a thing, except the doorbell," Dallas answered. "I checked around the side, and it looks like someone entered through the window. Probably ought to get pictures of that, too." He watched the two men interact, deciding they were brothers. "So you know Kira?"

"She's our sister." Garrett looked at Dallas.

Officer Richards joined the conversation. "When I heard her name, I suspected she could be related to you, but Dallas said she's African American."

"Yep, we adopted her when she was six."

"You were right, Officer Brooks," the young cop replied. "Do you want me to stick around or—"

"Yes," both brothers said.

The detective continued as he took pictures of the scraped up door with a muddy shoe tread on it. "We can't process our sister's case. It's officially yours, Richards. I just want to get pictures before anyone touches anything. You'll have to call in someone else to process. We're here as brothers, not officials."

"You haven't heard from her, either?" Dallas asked.

"She called a few days ago to apologize for missing my birthday," Garrett answered. "She said she'd had a bad week and forgot." He stepped aside as his brother returned from taking pictures of the window. "You have something to do with her bad week?"

Realization hit Dallas like a fist in the gut. This

was his fault, and Kira hadn't told anyone about what had happened. "Yeah," he said, "it was my fault. I've been trying to get hold of her all week. She wouldn't return my calls."

"And you have the nerve to show up here and put her name out over the entire region? That's a misuse of the system! We ought to write you up." Garrett stepped toward Dallas.

The detective pushed his brother back. "Calm down, Garrett. I don't think this was personal."

Garrett stood his ground. "What makes you think that?"

"He's not her type, for one thing. He's a cop. You really think she wants *another cop* in her life?" The detective put his gloves on. "So, give me the key."

His brother didn't move.

"Garrett. Let's see what's going on here and then we can jump to conclusions."

Dallas wanted to laugh, but this was too bizarre. Right now, he just wanted to know where their sister was, that she was okay. He'd deal with the second punch in the ego later.

Garrett glared at Dallas as he handed the keys over. It looked as if he was used to taking orders from his brother. So Nick was the arrogant detective, and Garrett the one with a temper. He probably had a chip on each shoulder. Dallas crossed his arms over his chest and met Garrett's stare, as if he could look inside and size the man up. A muscle flickered in Garrett's jaw. He was trying to prove himself, especially on the job. He was probably the younger of the two, though with his buzz cut, it was difficult to be sure.

Officer Richards leaned close. "So what *did* happen between you two?"

Dallas really didn't want to be the one to tell her brothers what had happened. She had her reasons for keeping it from them. "I came to get a statement for an incident that happened when she did a ride-along. I've phoned every day, but she's not returning my calls."

"You called in a BOLO just because she didn't phone you back?" Garrett eyed Dallas with a protective glare. "She didn't say anything about the ride-along when I talked to her."

"Mom said she'd been talking to someone about her new project." Nick looked at Dallas. "So what makes you think something is wrong, Brooks?"

Dallas wasn't getting anywhere with this tack. "I'm just worried. She doesn't seem like the type to not follow up on business."

"Follow up on what?"

"While I was inside the house that night talking to the mother and son, the mom's boyfriend must have been hiding in the backyard, and tried to break into the cruiser…with your sister inside."

Nick looked as if he wanted to punch him.

"I've done what I could to let her do this in her own timing," Dallas continued. "Now I need her statement so I can finish my report. I found out she's not been at work for days, she's not here, and I found the screen torn off one of her windows. The inside of her condo looks fairly torn up, too. That's when I called your officer in." The two brothers stared at Dallas in disbelief. "Are we going to stand here, or make sure Kira is okay?" he asked them.

"Yeah," Nick said, with a glare.

Dallas followed as they went inside. "This doesn't look good. Why'd she dump out her purse and leave it here?"

Garrett looked in the closet off the front door. Nick went to check the bedrooms, and Garrett went to the attached garage, while Dallas and the street cop searched the kitchen and living room.

"No sign of her in the bedroom," Nick yelled down the stairs, "but it looks like she went somewhere in a hurry. Her dresser drawers are hanging open."

"Is her suitcase gone?" Officer Richards asked.

"She doesn't have one. She borrows Mom's," Garrett answered as he came out of the garage with a puzzled look on his face. "Her car's still here. Maybe she's out on a date."

Dallas opened the microwave, surprised to find an overcooked and dried-out chicken pasta dinner. "With a broken window and a cooked, uneaten dinner in the microwave?" He couldn't imagine the woman he'd met the other night living in a mess like this. Jackets and shoes were scattered about.

"This isn't like Kira at all," Nick stated as he examined the other windows and the back door. "I'm going to call Mom, see if she knows anything."

"Who was this guy? The one that attacked her?" Garrett asked while Nick talked into his phone.

"Attacked the car. He didn't touch her. Drug dealer, goes by Mickey Zelanski. He had a stash of coke as big as Kira's kitchen."

Garrett started with the attitude again. "So he attacks the car she's in and you let him go? Nice work."

Dallas felt the hair on his neck tingle. "She sounded the siren and scared him away. He was gone by the time I got out there. Crazy me, I wanted to make sure your sister was okay."

"Why didn't she call you on the radio?"

"She did, but it didn't sound anything like your sister, trust me." Dallas didn't need this. "You want answers, Garrett, get Kira to come fill out a statement. Then we'll both know what she went through out there."

That wasn't good enough, apparently. Though the attitude mellowed, Garrett kept pressing for information. "And why didn't she fill it out that night?"

"Knock it off, I can't hear Mom," Nick yelled.

"What about Kira?" Garrett asked.

Nick gave a thumbs-up. A couple of minutes later, he joined them. "Kira's okay. She's been at Mom and Dad's the last few days."

Dallas let out a deep breath, along with her brothers.

These two might not be Kira's blood, but there was no doubt how they felt about her.

"Mom said she seems okay, but it doesn't sound like Kira told them anything, either. Dad's bringing her over to confirm whether someone else has been in here, or what in the world got hold of our neat-freak sister."

Dallas appreciated that his first impression of her was accurate, but that didn't sound good for her emotional state of mind right now. Her sarcasm echoed through his head: *I'm fine, they're fine, everyone is fine. That's what you want, right?* He had hoped she was strong enough that the incident wouldn't have bothered her. Looks like he was wrong. He should have followed Shaline's suggestion and come to see her right away.

While the brothers talked to the officer, Dallas wandered the room, trying to understand Kira a little better. She had a lot of family pictures mixed in with simple decorations. Candles, bowls with dried flowers and leaves in them. Very few trinkets, he noted.

"Look at this," the street officer said. "What was this burglar looking for?" In the hallway, books had been knocked off the shelf, videos tossed into the trash. The pictures on the wall were crooked, but nothing of any value appeared to be missing. The television and computer hadn't been bothered.

Dallas kept quiet, allowing the brothers to determine what was out of place.

If it was Zelanski, what had he been looking for? Why would he bother Kira? Unless he thought she had taken something besides the kids' belongings…

As Dallas walked back into the living room, her computer monitor flashed on. "Someone has definitely been here recently," he stated. "I bumped the desk, and the computer came right up." He leaned down to read the error message. "Someone was trying to get into her computer, but didn't have a password."

The detective joined him. "Good work, Officer."

"Dallas," he corrected.

"Am I going to find your prints on this?" the man challenged, pulling a pen from his pocket to point to the mouse.

"I know how to handle a crime investigation, Detective."

"What about the rest of the apartment? Your fingerprints anywhere else?" Garrett Matthews asked.

Dallas glared at the young street officer. His response was cut off by yet another voice, this one even deeper than her brothers'. "Kira Danae. What happened here?" An older version of the well-dressed detective walked into the room. Their dad.

Dallas waited anxiously to see Kira again, his thoughts flashing back to the night they'd met. For a moment, he wanted the impossible—to start all over again.

Kira covered her mouth and choked back a cry when she saw her house. Then she came face-to-face with Dallas. A flash of fury had the color returning to her cheeks. Her brown eyes were wide and round, a sure sign that she was about to let him have it.

That's what the bulletproof vest was for—to protect his heart from a lethal shot. And this woman certainly had the ammunition to do the job. Heart. Spunk. And blind faith. That was the problem with social workers, he realized as she lit into him. They thought they could heal everyone. And unfortunately, he was one that just couldn't be healed.

She stared point-blank at Dallas and spoke through gritted teeth. "Next time I want my family to know about my life, I'd appreciate it if you'd let *me* tell them."

He stared into her eyes, analyzing her reaction. "You'd better start talking, then, because I don't think your brothers like my version."

NINE

"What are you doing here?" Kira narrowed her eyes.

"You know why I'm here." Dallas's gaze came to rest on her, and she felt the same warmth she had that night. "I needed to talk to you about the case." How did Dallas expect to look at her that way without giving the impression he was interested?

"You put out a BOLO on me!" Kira bit out the accusation while her two brothers and her father stood guard. Maybe that meant Dallas did care.

"No, don't—" Before he could respond, her oldest brother stormed through the door.

"Kira, I was at the jail and heard your name. What's going on?" He looked around, apparently surprised to see most of the family. "Are you okay?" Kent asked, wrapping one arm around her. He was looking even scruffier than usual, even for an undercover job in narcotics.

"I'm fi—" she began, stealing a glance at Dallas's clenched jaw. Then she changed her answer, "No, I'm not. I've been better, but I'm not hurt." She closed her eyes, steadying herself in her brother's embrace. She couldn't believe they had all showed up.

This was not going to be easy to explain.

She felt a tap on her shoulder. "We should move outside, let investigators do what they can to get prints," her dad suggested. "You're going to need to answer some questions about your apartment, too." He glanced at Dallas. "The rest of you boys may as well get back to work. I'll take care of Kira."

Kira paused at the doorway for another look. She couldn't believe someone had actually broken into her house. Had that lunatic been watching her all week? Maybe she hadn't been hearing things, after all. She gazed at Dallas as he introduced himself to her oldest brother.

She should feel guilty for snapping at Dallas, she told herself, but she didn't. She wasn't ready to talk to him, because that meant it was time to review everything that had happened. For two days, she'd been able to block all of that from her mind.

Her dad and brothers were pacing outside the condo with the local officer, making sure nothing was missed. She heard them ticking off things that were out of place, wondering how they could know her so well. She wrapped her arms around herself and rubbed her skin to warm herself up.

Dallas walked into her condo and emerged with a

jacket barely a minute later. "You look a little cold, and since my jacket is in the car outside the gate…" He waved his arms.

"It's *that* way," Kira corrected. "Just so you don't get lost when you go to leave."

"How thoughtful of you," he said with a wry smile. "Anyway, I talked them into clearing one of your jackets for you."

"Thanks," she said. *You can't be so nice and then walk away, leaving me miserable again, Dallas. Keep your guard up, Kira.*

Dallas glanced around, then tucked his thumbs into his pockets. "So, do you have any more brothers?"

She felt a sinking feeling as she remembered a little boy as he was torn away from her. She nodded. "Yes, but he's not a cop, and he won't be showing up here, that I can assure you."

Dallas smiled, "If I'd known you were related to half the force over here…well, it would have simplified things."

"You call this simple?" Her brothers were stalling, studying her and Dallas. Probably waiting for the full scoop.

Dallas turned his back to the men and squinted at her critically. "I was worried when you didn't return my calls. It's been nearly a week. One message and we could've avoided this scene."

Kira wrapped her arms around her body once more,

trying to escape the chill that was taking over again. "I can't explain."

"You'd better try," Dallas retorted.

"Whoa, whoa, whoa, time out here." Kent said as he approached, holding his hands in a T in front of him. "All of this is about a date gone bad?"

Suddenly everyone was back in the driveway, looking at them.

"What?" Kira and Dallas said in unison.

Kira's face flushed. "No, this isn't about—"

Dallas interrupted her. "It's a small misunderstanding about a statement for an incident report. But it seems that the incident has led to more problems." He moved the focus back to her condo, and her brothers took over the conversation again. Kira was bombarded with questions about who would have done this to her, why, when….

"Wait just a minute," she finally blurted out, clearly overwhelmed by all the attention. "What makes you think someone targeted me? I've been gone for two days. Maybe they just—"

"This wasn't a crime of opportunity, Kira. They didn't take anything of value. They were looking for something specific," Nick interrupted. "This officer came a long way out of his jurisdiction to make sure you're okay. So if your not calling him back has nothing to do with a bad date, why don't you start by telling us what *did* happen."

"Could we talk alone for a minute?" Dallas suggested quietly as he turned to Kira.

She nodded. Anything to avoid the inevitable.

He took hold of her arm with gentle authority, leading her to the end of the driveway. He released her immediately when she began to pull away.

Dallas's eyes seemed deeper set, and concern etched his face. "I know what you're going through. You don't want to think about it any more than necessary, especially not when it means telling your family. Fact remains, they're not going to let it go now, and I need to get your statement."

She tucked her arms into her jacket and noticed her brothers working hard to listen to her conversation with Dallas. She turned her back on her family and whispered, "Let's take a walk around the block."

Though his eyebrows furrowed, Dallas told her brothers, "We'll be right back."

Garrett jumped forward instantly. "You're not—"

Kira glared him, letting Dallas stand between them. "Knock it off, Garrett, he's a cop. Nothing's going to happen to me."

Dallas touched her arm and they headed down the street. "You don't really believe they're going to let you off the hook, do you?"

"No, but maybe Dad'll send them back to work. I need more time to decide what I want to tell them." Kira looked over her shoulder to make sure none of them had followed. "I know I have to tell them something, but I don't know how much they need to know. Isn't it confidential or something?"

"Not if it happened to you. You can tell who you want. You don't have to, but you can. Kira, you can't make all of this go away by ignoring it. What happened was not your fault. I'll make sure they know that."

"You keep saying you know what I'm going through," she said. "You can't know. You can't know how it felt to be trapped with a lunatic after me," she insisted, fighting her inclination to raise her voice. She expected Dallas to interrupt, but he remained silent, probably waiting for her to calm down again. "I could have been the one going into that house alone, without a gun, without a radio to call for backup." She pointed to herself.

He didn't argue.

"I thought I was fine, but when I got home…" Her voice gave out. She couldn't explain how difficult this week had been for her.

"The shadows start talking, don't they?"

She was afraid to look at him and let him know he was right. "I can't tell them what happened, Officer Brooks."

"Call me Dallas. You seem to forget that you're the victim here, not the guilty party." His voice was calm and quiet. "I blame myself every bit as much as you do for leaving you in harm's way. And you're probably going to be even madder at me, because I told your brothers some of what happened in order to get them to understand my concern that your condo looked suspicious. I wanted them to stop acting like this was some lover's spat. Before you, your dad and the narcotics officer arrived, the detective and the hothead thought I broke your heart. Right about now, I wish it *was* just a personal fight between us."

"What?" Had this guy lost his mind, too?

He took hold of her hand and she spun to a stop in front of him. "I do, because then you wouldn't be hearing shadows talking. Because then we wouldn't have so much in common. Because then I wouldn't be afraid for your safety." He let go of her hand and stared at her. Kira backed away, stopped by the granite sign of the subdivision. "I know you don't want anyone to know how afraid you are, Kira. You want to be the same strong woman you were before that night. I'm going to tell you that isn't going to happen. Especially not in a matter of a week or two."

"That's really comforting." She looked at him in disbelief as he stood with his arms crossed over his broad chest. He looked every bit as sturdy as the granite rock she leaned against.

"No, it's not. Neither is ignoring it. Or denial. I'm not sure yet where you're at with what happened, but it's not going to get any better until you face it. I should have followed my sergeant's advice that night. He told me to go get you and bring you back, but I was being selfish. I wasn't about to have to admit to anyone that I'm not a tough ex-cop from Phoenix. It's taken me over three years to get here tonight, to admit that I live with post-traumatic stress disorder. You're the first and only person besides my supervisor that I've ever told. So you're wrong, I know exactly what you're going through."

She didn't know what to say. "What happened?"

"Too much to go into right now, but I want to tell you about it sometime so you can realize I do know what you're going through. You can hide, but the shadows keep coming back. The sooner you deal with it and let your loved ones help you through it, the sooner you'll get better." Dallas pointed behind him. "You have brothers down the block who dropped everything to make sure you're okay. They want you to be okay, just as much as you do—just as much as I do."

Kira started walking again, not wanting to face any of this. Surely if she went far enough, it wouldn't find her. Unfortunately, Dallas wasn't going to let it go. "Things like this don't happen to my brothers. They won't understand, especially when they find out what a pansy I am." Kira picked up the pace until she rounded the bend and once again saw her brothers and dad pacing in front of her condo. She slowed down, torn between facing them and listening to Dallas's soft, firm voice like a shadow behind her, making her face reality.

"A pansy wouldn't have kept fighting for survival, searching for a way to save herself. She wouldn't have jumped right back into her job to protect two victimized children from that man," Dallas argued. "None of us knows how we'll handle a situation until we're thrown into it."

She was weary from thinking of this, running over it night and day for a week. "I thought I knew, though. I should have been prepared. I've lived on both sides of this incident, and I was still caught off guard."

"Every day God opens our eyes to learning something new. No matter how much training we go through, something is going to catch us off guard eventually. I ran away from law enforcement, didn't believe I'd ever be able to wear a uniform again. I'm a much better officer than I was before my incident. Maybe seeing how a victim's life is affected will help you and your brothers in some way, too."

She couldn't stop the tears. "I've always been a nuisance to them, from day one. They brought me home right before Garrett's birthday, and instead of getting a puppy, he got a little sister. You can imagine how thrilled he was with that."

Dallas laughed, a soft, unassuming chuckle that warmed her through. "I wouldn't worry about Garrett. It didn't seem to warp him too much. He seems to have some pretty protective genes in him."

Kira groaned, wiping the tears away. "They all do. I'll never live alone again after this."

"For a while, that may be a good thing. Which reminds me, you have a statement to give." He paused. "How do you want to deal with that? Ignoring it is not an option."

She shook her head.

"Just one warning. I'm not leaving tonight without it. I could make you come to the station with me, write it all out. I take the official copy, and you live with them hounding you forever about what really happened."

She winced. That was the coward's way out, and if she didn't tell her brothers now, they'd think it was much worse than it really was. "No, I'll tell them." She looked down the block at her family. "See, I'm fine."

"Good. Let me get my recorder, if you don't mind. It'll save you having to write it all out."

She nodded.

"The other thing we'll need to do is talk to the police here, work with them on who could have broken into your place. We both have a pretty good idea who did it, and I think you need to talk to your supervisor, maybe pair up with someone for a while, at least until we catch Mickey."

When Dallas returned, Kira had everyone gathered on the back porch, away from curious neighbors. She took that difficult journey into the shadows, comforted by the occasional question from Dallas that kept her going. Only once did Garrett try to interrupt. Dallas held his hand out, silencing him instantly.

Dallas asked her a few questions to fill in the gaps in his report. Then Kira faced the questions from the local police about her town house.

The officer handling the investigation asked for the

name of the man who had attacked the car. "Mickey Zelanski," Dallas responded.

"Why would he want anything in my house?" Kira still didn't understand.

"You're the only person who can identify him. His girlfriend is in jail, the DEA has taken his supply, and maybe he wants re—" Dallas stopped himself. "Who else would break in, but not take anything of value?"

"Nick?" Kira turned to the plainclothes brother. "Is that right? You think this is linked?"

He nodded. "Dallas's theory makes sense. Maybe Zelanski thinks you have something, records for instance. And yeah, maybe he just wants you out of the way. We can't ignore that possibility, as ugly as it is."

Kent was already on the phone. "Find out where Zelanski is for me, would you? And get hold of that DEA agent who dropped by the other day."

"Kent? You know that monster? Please tell me Zelanski isn't an undercover officer on your narcotics squad." Fire lit in Kira's soft brown eyes. "I might have to take him on myself if he is."

"No, he's not one of ours. But let me put it this way. you're not going anywhere alone until we have him behind bars."

Kira's dad pulled Kira to him and looked Dallas in the eye. "You keep us up-to-date on this case, Brooks. We'll do whatever we need to do to keep my little girl safe."

Dallas nodded at him and smiled. "Will do, sir. I'm

moving to the day shift as of tomorrow, but I'll still be following this case. Kira, I want to talk to you more about the incident."

Her father cleared his throat. "I'm going to make sure the house is locked up before we head home, Kira. Dallas, we'll see you again, I'm sure. Boys, you'd better get back to work."

Nick started to protest, but her dad herded them all through the house.

Kira's brothers took the hint and said goodbye, too. It was just her and Dallas now. "You were saying?"

"I want to discuss this, as one PTSD survivor to another, since you're not interested in dating a cop."

"Since I'm not...? Where did you get the impression I'm not interested in dating a cop?"

He paused a moment, then got a look of panic in his eyes. "You said so, and your brothers also told me."

She couldn't think of what she'd said to give him that impression, but it didn't surprise her that Nick and Garrett were against Dallas. They had always tried to scare off her dates.

"That's fine with me," Dallas added. "I don't want to pressure you. I just think that talking with someone who's been through the stress you have might be helpful. Are you free for dinner tomorrow night?"

"Yeah, maybe it would." Maybe it was best to get the romantic notions out of her mind for now.

Dallas seemed almost relieved by the announcement.

Was he afraid of getting involved? Kira's heart raced at the memories of him comforting her after the incident with Mickey.

"Let me give you my parents' address and I'll see you tomorrow." She didn't dare let her guard down, did she? Or was God trying to show her the silver lining to this horrible week?

TEN

The only thing pushing Dallas to step inside the high school at six twenty-five the next morning was his motivation to make it to six that evening to see Kira again. He wasn't worried about her in the same way he had been twenty-four hours ago, but he still couldn't get his mind off her.

He tried to convince himself that it was because he felt at least partially to blame for her suffering. His conscience wouldn't let him rest until he tried to help her through this. Any other reason would be a huge mistake. Relationships and post-traumatic stress disorder mixed about as well as oil and water. Add to that the lousy statistics for police officers' divorce rates, and getting involved with Miss Matthews was out of the question.

Definitely out of the question.

He took a deep breath, muttered a small prayer and found a custodian who directed him to Brad

Johnson's office. Dallas was surprised to find a pair of crutches propped next to the senior ranking officer's desk.

"What happened to you?" Dallas asked.

"An old knee injury flared up after a mishap painting the house last weekend." Johnson shook his head and stood up. "I'm sure after a couple of weeks of therapy, it's going to be good as new."

"I hope so," Dallas said. He wished he could be as confident as Johnson. Even if he was better, he wasn't likely to be in good enough shape to qualify to be on duty in a matter of weeks. "So how about we get busy here. Show me around. Tell me what to watch for…."

"It's been a pretty quiet year," the officer began, and kept talking as he gathered his crutches to give Dallas the tour. Brad introduced Dallas to the principal and staff. Antelope Springs High School was home to almost five hundred students, nowhere near the enrollment they had at the school Dallas had been at in Phoenix. Even so, it wasn't comforting to think he had less than one-fourth the students to monitor.

Brad hobbled through the school, pointing out the emergency exits and potential weak areas where they had recurrent security problems. Dallas could understand why they had wanted someone who was familiar with the job requirements. To anyone new, going through the building's crisis manual in a matter of hours would seem like preparing for Pearl Harbor on a day's notice.

"Hey, Johnson," a tall kid said, stopping them in the hallway. "Is this the new SRO?"

Brad came to a stop and leaned on his crutches with a sigh. "Yeah. Tucker, this is Officer Brooks. I've warned him about you," he joked.

Dallas recalled those days, making friends with the students. At one time, he'd loved being their role model, their friend, a person they could come to when they needed an ear. He'd loved keeping them out of trouble.

"Hey, Brooks." The youth raised his fist, waiting for Dallas to tap knuckles.

"That's *Officer* Brooks," Dallas corrected. *Don't let the kid get to you. Remember Alek was a friend, too.* Reluctantly, Dallas ignored the student's attempt to get connected. He wasn't here to make friends. "The late bell's about to ring. Do you have class this period?"

The kid nodded, a puzzled look on his face. "Yeah, I'm going." He glanced at Johnson, who simply tilted his head, motioning down the hall. Tucker seemed disappointed as he walked to the classroom two doors away.

Didn't Officer Johnson normally push the kids to get to class on time?

Brad looked at Dallas, a smirk on his face. "He likes to hang out in my office and talk. He's a good kid, but school's boring for him."

"Yeah, it might be a little more interesting if he tried a little harder. My office won't be a hangout."

Johnson paused a minute. "Whatever works for you,"

he said, then moved on with the tour. An hour later, he said goodbye and headed out, leaving Dallas in one of his dreaded discussions with the shadows.

As he walked the halls, studying the layout of the school, he couldn't help but relate to Kira's emotional state. He hadn't been inside a school in over three years and he didn't want to be here now. He wanted to be anywhere but here, where kids' voices echoed in his head. Some jokesters. Most friendly. One, an angry loner, dead set on revenge—all over a few days suspension. That was the loudest voice, drowning out all the others. One "friend" who had turned on Dallas when the system didn't give in to his plan.

Dallas's breathing quickened. His heartbeat echoed in his ears. His determination to keep to himself grew stronger. He was here to keep the kids safe, not to be liked, or be cool, or help the kids succeed. Nope, he wouldn't make that mistake twice.

Each hour, as the end of each period approached, Dallas became a visible fixture in one of the hallways. During class, he kept an eye on one of the entrances. Watching, studying. All except the front doors were supposed to be locked, yet he constantly saw students opening the side entrances to let other students come and go. He made a note to talk to the principal. His list of concerns grew longer each hour. *Things are way too lax here.* Why had these issues not been addressed earlier? It was past spring break.

When the final bell rang, Dallas watched students storm the exits. He waited outside, watching traffic, waiting to be needed, thankful when he wasn't.

Before he left for the day, he stopped by the main office. "Is the principal in?"

"He's in meetings for the rest of the afternoon, Officer Brooks." The receptionist looked barely old enough to be out of high school herself. "By the way, I'm Candy Carson." She leaned against the tall counter across from Dallas and twirled her hair around her finger. "Would you like to schedule a meeting with him?"

Dallas placed his hands on the edge of the counter and pushed away from the girl as she inched closer. "If that's the best way to block out an hour or two of his schedule, then yes, Miss Carson."

"Two hours?" She raised her eyebrows. "Wow, that sounds serious. Is there a problem?"

He didn't have the patience to deal with this, today or ever. "Not if I can help it. Is he available in the morning, or would after school fit into his schedule better?" Dallas stared into her eyes, hoping she'd realize he was ignoring her blatant flirtation.

She went to her computer and leaned over the keyboard, apparently not minding that he was ignoring her.

Dallas turned to read the announcement board while Miss Carson punched keys. "Huh," she said, and Dallas glanced over his shoulder just as she bit her lip and batted her eyelashes. "His day is pretty full tomorrow.

Maybe if you come back in the morning, he can fit you in for a few minutes."

"I'll send him an e-mail. Thanks, anyway." He slapped a hand on the counter and walked to the exit.

"See you in the morning," she said as he walked out the door.

Dallas returned to his office and shot an e-mail to the principal requesting a meeting ASAP to discuss security as outlined in the building's crisis manual.

He felt as if the weight of the world was lifted off his shoulders when he walked out the door and got into the patrol car to head back to the station. Once there, he took his bulletproof vest off and changed into his street clothes. Layer by layer, he felt more human and vulnerable, missing the protection the uniform offered.

He was ready to leave when his cell phone rang. Kira's brother Kent was calling to say his contacts hadn't seen Mickey in almost two weeks, but the fingerprints lifted from Kira's condo matched. And for Dallas, the inner turmoil began again.

As he headed to Fossil Creek to pick up Kira, he watched to be sure he wasn't being followed. He had no clue where to go for dinner. He wanted someplace where they could have privacy to talk, as he didn't want their issues and feelings to be overheard. Most of the restaurants he could think of were either so busy that they would have to struggle to hear one another, or the setting would lead her to the wrong conclusion. While she was just the kind of woman he would like to date, he couldn't take the chance. He didn't want to get off on the wrong foot and set her brothers off again.

He found her parents' house without much problem, parked his car along the curb and took a deep breath. He struggled to keep reins on the anticipation of talking with Kira tonight. *Don't forget, this isn't a date.*

Before he could ring the doorbell, a dog barked on the other side of the door. A yippy little dog, from the sound of it. Kira's dad answered with a small white fluff ball in his arms. "Evening, Dallas." Ted managed to make himself heard above the high-pitched barking of the excited animal. "Excuse Pom Pom. She's our alarm system."

Dallas laughed. "Is it a happy yip, or is she ready to attack?"

"Depends on if she likes the visitor," her dad said as the dog nearly wiggled out of his arms to get to Dallas. She couldn't weigh more than six pounds, two of it fur.

"I see. I'll try to keep on her good side then." Dallas let the dog sniff his hand, and the friendship began. "How's Kira today?" He stepped inside and closed the door, expecting her to appear at any moment.

"Doing pretty well. I wanted to make a suggestion. I'm a little concerned about her being out in the public before Zelanski is caught," he said, his voice gruff.

Dallas was ready to argue when her dad continued. "Turns out her office received threatening calls wanting to know where those kids are. They advised Kira to stay home a few more days to let the police trace the calls."

"So Zelanski does want something that the kids have," Dallas stated thoughtfully aloud. "I knew it."

Kira rushed down the stairs, renewing Dallas's worry. This crazy man would do whatever it took, even if it meant hurting an innocent woman to get what he wanted.

"Hi," she said, with a somber smile.

Does she know about the calls? Dallas felt better just having the chance to spend some time talking with her. "Evening." He tried to hide his admiration, as Kira's father was still watching him.

"Dallas, Grace and I would feel a lot better if you two had dinner here tonight."

"Dad," Kira said in disbelief. "I said I would talk to him about it."

"Fine, talk to him then. I'm going to go get changed for my date. Unless you want us to stay home." Ted put the dog down and it jumped as if it had springs for legs.

Dinner with her parents was out of the question. Dallas wasn't going to get anywhere discussing what had happened, not with them around. Kira had hardly given her father the bare facts last night. He looked at her father, realizing the older man was waiting for his response, his hand on the banister. "Thank you for the offer, Mr. Matthews…"

"There are steaks in the fridge, and we thought you

could grill them and have some privacy here. That is, unless you had other plans."

"Dad…" Kira said. "Just go. We'll be fine, whether we go out or stay here."

"I'm going, I'm going!" Ted muttered as he disappeared up the staircase.

Despite his discomfort at accepting her father's somewhat domineering hospitality, Dallas wondered if doing so wasn't best. That way Kira wouldn't get any misconceptions about why he had asked her to dinner. And since she had no interest in dating, he wouldn't be concerned with choosing too cozy of a restaurant. "Either is fine with me, Kira. What do you want to do?"

Her smile hinted at her loneliness, a feeling that Dallas could understand all too well. "This case seems to have the tentacles of an octopus, and I'll admit, I am a little shaken by it. We need to talk, and I don't think either of us will be comfortable opening up in a public place," she said.

"That was my concern, too. I wouldn't have suggested we stay here, but I'm fine with it if it makes you more comfortable."

"You really don't mind?" Her surprise was obvious. "I mean, thank you, Dallas. I would definitely be more comfortable at home…Mom and Dad's home."

Before he knew it, he'd wrapped an arm around her shoulder. "I don't mind, really." Dallas didn't like that he was caring more and more for Kira, let alone worrying about how every decision would affect her.

As if Kira had read his mind, her dark brown eyes softened as she admired him. "Would you mind helping with your dinner?"

The subtle exchange set off alarms of old fears and uncertainties. He followed her down a wide hallway that opened up to a formal dining room with candles and fresh flowers on the table. Someone apparently hadn't gotten the same message he had about Kira's disinterest in dating cops. *How am I going to get out of this one?*

He'd been torn between pushing to get Kira back into a normal routine, and wanting to protect her like her family was doing. After the shooting in Phoenix he had wanted to lock himself away from everyone: his fiancée, family, life in general. But in his case, the individual intent on hurting people was out of the picture. In her case, he was still a very real threat.

Kira continued to the kitchen, where she handed him a knife and a small loaf of French bread. "If you'll butter the bread, I'll make a salad," she said, as if they were an ordinary couple.

"Sure," he answered, trying to squelch his inclination to care about her. She looked happy tearing lettuce and chopping tomatoes, doing the routine things that couples normally did together.

Dallas's chest tightened. Why he had this reaction every time he saw her, he couldn't understand. He hadn't been interested in dating in three years, not since Jessica had broken their engagement. Since then, he hadn't met one woman he'd wanted to date casually, let alone seriously. Less than a year into his new career, and he couldn't seem to get his mind off the one woman who wanted nothing to do with a police officer. Just his luck.

Her parents stepped into the room, and Dallas felt like an awkward teenager on a first date. Kira quickly introduced him to her mom, Grace, before her dad rushed them out the door, claiming they'd be late for the play if they didn't hurry.

While Kira set the salad in the refrigerator and Dallas finished buttering the bread, an awkward silence stretched between them. He wrapped the bread in the foil that it was on, and Kira set it in the warm oven. She turned around, her gaze roaming from his chest to his face.

"You sure you don't mind eating here?"

He couldn't stop analyzing her, and apparently she was doing a bit of analysis on herself.

He nodded. "I'm sure. So what have you been doing all week?" Pom Pom yipped as they pulled the steak out of the refrigerator, and guarded Kira at the grill.

Kira smiled at the pup, consoling her with a doggy treat. Again, Dallas felt an odd rhythm in his chest. "Not much, until today," she told him. "Dad drove Mom and me to my office, where I tried to get some work done."

"And?"

"Every time the phone rang, Mom jumped a mile

and asked a hundred questions. It wasn't worth it. I brought my paperwork home." Kira opened a cabinet and pulled out plates, handing them to him. "Would you set them on the table over there?" She nodded toward a sizable table across the kitchen, and Dallas breathed a sigh of relief.

"Were you afraid we were going to eat in the dining room with the candles and flowers?" Kira laughed softly and he realized his sigh must not have been mental.

"What, are you a detective now, or a mind reader?"

Kira laughed again. "I'd say it's in my blood, but I guess that's pretty obviously not it, right? I guess I just have too many brothers to not recognize panic when I see it."

He'd only met her a week ago. But he couldn't seem to get her out of his head. She was going to capture his heart if he wasn't careful.

ELEVEN

Kira had waited patiently while they ate dinner, and still she knew little more than she had when Dallas arrived. She glanced across the large round table, wondering if she should have sat farther away, but that seemed so cold. Then again, sitting next to Dallas may have made him uncomfortable. Maybe that's why he'd been so quiet.

He's quiet because he's not interested. "More tea?" Kira offered. She didn't want to seem pushy, but she did want to correct him on one major point. He was hurting, and she wanted nothing more than to help him through it.

"Sure," he said as he held out his glass.

She struggled to keep her mind on pouring and not on his muscular forearms. Or his blue eyes, which were the color of the Caribbean, and a definite distraction. His military buzz cut was typical of most street cops, but slightly overgrown.

She took a nibble of bread and felt the silence stretch

dangerously thin. "This isn't getting us very far, is it? And here I thought being in a quiet house would make it easier."

"I'm sorry," Dallas said, pushing his empty plate away. "I'm not sure where to start." He looked Kira in the eyes and she felt his pain as well as her own.

"Maybe some dessert would help. We happen to have a choice tonight—chocolate cake or cheesecake."

"A tough choice. How about I think about it while we do dishes," he said as he stood. "I'll wash, and since you know where the dishes belong, you can put things away."

She really didn't want to bother with dishes right now, but she also realized how much better an interview with clients went when they were busy and had a distraction. "Okay," she said, filling the sink with soap and water, while Dallas added the dishes. She glanced at the dishwasher, resisting the temptation to roll her eyes. Doing the few dishes that they had dirtied wasn't going to buy him much time. "So, I believe you promised to tell me about an experience of yours?"

He shook the bubbles from his hands and leaned back against the counter. "You've got to realize I haven't talked to anyone about this before," he said. "Well, no one that I wasn't required to talk to. None of my friends knew. My fiancée didn't want to hear it, and when she finally did, she couldn't deal with it. A couple months later she broke our engagement."

Kira wasn't sure how to respond. "From what I've read about post-traumatic stress disorder, that's fairly common."

"Yeah, it is. She gave me a choice, my career or her. Some days I still wonder if this is really what God wanted me to do."

"What do you mean?"

"Return to law enforcement. I took a few years off after my incident, tried other jobs. Before I decided to apply for another police position, God and I had some lengthy discussions. I had some serious doubts, and a few stipulations." He glanced over to Kira. "Lately, it seems the rules of our agreement have changed."

She studied him for a minute. "You…negotiated…with God?"

Dallas gave a small chuckle. "Sounds pretty ridiculous when you say it that way, doesn't it?"

Kira shrugged. "I didn't mean that the way it came out. I've just never thought of those frequent prayers I have as 'negotiations.' I always sort of felt like whatever God wanted, I needed to do."

Dallas smiled. "Well, that explains why I ended up back in law-enforcement then, doesn't it?"

"Not necessarily. I'm no expert."

"It's been a lot more difficult to keep in touch lately. With God, I mean." He paused. "It was so much easier when I worked normal hours. When I went through treatment, I felt so close. I attended church on a fairly regular basis, and, well, when you're working low-stress jobs, life's just a little easier to swallow. But I wasn't happy, and my fiancée insisted I wasn't the same person anymore."

Kira looked away, not wanting to point out to Dallas that it may have been a blessing in disguise. He certainly wouldn't have been here if God hadn't meant for him to return to police work. "As you said, after a crisis, you're never going to be the same person. Why don't we sit down in the family room." Maybe Dallas was simply here tonight to satisfy his supervisor. Maybe he had no personal interest in her at all. "Do you mind if I ask about your incident?"

"That is why I'm here, isn't it?" he said with a grimace. He paused in the doorway as Kira let the dog outside. "I was a police officer for four years in Phoenix, so there were plenty of opportunities for disaster. What finally did me in was a year and a half working as a school resource officer, or SRO, as we call them here. I had a great time. It was rewarding to feel like I made a difference, which was sometimes the discouraging part of being a patrolman in a big city."

Kira edged past Dallas and pointed toward the cozy family room. "I can understand that. It is a huge city."

"Yes, it is. At the school, the kids and I built a rapport, and even in the evenings, they called if they were in a situation they couldn't handle. It was good to feel needed, almost like being more of a big brother than a security officer."

Kira smiled. "Cody seemed to connect with you immediately the other night, but you didn't seem too thrilled."

Dallas shrugged. "Yeah. And I don't think Cody was that thrilled with me, either. If a dog had bitten Mickey and gotten rid of him, Cody would have thanked the dog, too."

She laughed, and elbowed Dallas playfully. Though she knew he was being modest, Kira had seen that Cody was drawn to Dallas, despite his denial.

Dallas took a deep breath and slowly let it out.

"Let's go sit in an easy chair," Kira suggest. She sat on the sofa and tucked her feet under her other leg.

"There was this young man that I'd gone out of the way for, on many occasions." Dallas said, turning serious again. He sat next to Kira and continued talking. "He was a troubled kid, and I felt for him. Parents were split, both too busy with their successful careers to keep an eye on the boy. He had become a truancy problem, but he promised me he'd work harder. He would come into my office and do his homework. He was improving his grades, but he had a long way to go."

Dallas's voice cracked, and Kira felt her heart squeeze tighter. She wanted to make his pain go away, just as he did hers. Her mind ran wild with possibilities of what could have happened next. Dallas didn't speak for the longest time. Kira finally offered to get him more iced tea.

He shook his head. "I'm okay." He took a deep breath. "Something snapped. The kid had a string of incidents. I talked with him every day, trying to figure out what was going on. Then one day his girlfriend broke up with him, and Alek got into a fight with a classmate he thought was to blame for the breakup." Dallas leaned his elbows on his knees and put his head in his hands.

"The principal gave him a five-day suspension to cool down. After lunch four days later, his teacher called the principal's office, reporting that Alek was back in class, being very disruptive and acting strange. I got a page to report to the classroom, but by the time I got there, the teacher had sent him to the office. The kids in the class were upset, and rumors were rampant. Someone claimed he had a bomb in his backpack."

Kira covered her mouth, fearing what had happened next.

"When I met up with him in the main lobby, he had a gun and was demanding to see the principal."

Dallas slipped into a trancelike state, reciting the events as if he'd gone through them a million times. He probably had, Kira thought.

"I was at the opposite end of the main building and caught up with Alek as he reached the office. The bell rang, and a friend of his came out of class and saw Al-Alek with a semiautomatic pistol. Even his best friend couldn't talk him down."

Kira held her breath. Her heart raced.

"He shot several times, and one bullet ricocheted

and hit the friend in the knee. That made Alek mad, and he turned on me, as if he blamed me for that shot. He fired once at me, then turned to shoot the principal as he walked out of the office.

Kira gasped, and she instinctively rubbed his shoulders.

"Alek fired again." Dallas's voice caught. "He missed. I didn't."

Kira felt hiss muscles twitch with each word. "Oh, Dallas," she cried softly. She offered her hand, and he quietly took hold of it. "Wh-who?" she stammered. "Who was shot, and how bad was he hurt?"

"Alek," Dallas whispered, with a shake of his head. "He didn't make it through the night."

Kira sat in stunned silence. Instinctively, she cocooned his hand in both of hers. How could she have ever let her experience with Mickey become so over-blown? She waited for Dallas to continue the story, but he didn't. "What about his friend? And the principal? Are they okay?"

"The friend had an athletic scholarship, before the shooting. After the injury he just wasn't the same. He took a break, but he did go to college and is going to earn his degree. The principal wasn't injured."

Kira shook her head. "I feel ridiculous for overreacting to the incident with Mickey. I'm so sorry, Dallas."

He looked her in the eye, sadness replaced with peace. He had pulled out of the past and was back in the room with her again. "You weren't overreacting, Kira.

You still aren't. Mickey is a serious threat to your safety. Don't ever ignore your gut instincts."

"I'm not, but I can't just check out of living and my responsibility, either."

"Fear is sometimes a protective mechanism. Both of us reacted more to the realization of what could have happened. While taking a young boy's life was horrible, what haunts me is that it could have been worse. He'd been in trouble several times. We cut him a little slack, and I worked with him, probably more than I should have…" His voice faded away.

She let out a heavy sigh. "Don't doubt your good intentions, Dallas. You tried to help. There's no way it could have been too much. God knows that."

He shrugged. "I kept trying to make up for something he'd missed along the way." Dallas's grip tightened on Kira's hand. "Maybe it wasn't too much for him, but it was for me." He clenched his jaw and twisted his mouth. "You're probably thinking of what Mickey may have done to hurt these kids. Maybe you're angry that someone didn't stop him earlier, knowing that the DEA was watching him."

Kira shook her head. "Not only that, I found out my brother's team has been watching Mickey for weeks. They hoped he would lead them to his supplier." She let out a soft growl. "Kent claims Mickey had a residence that he was using as a decoy. This one was a total surprise."

"I'd like to believe him," Dallas stated.

"I'm beginning to think it's more comforting to believe him than the truth." She shook her head. She couldn't help that she was an idealist living among pessimistic realists. She knew from experience that cops saw more reality than most individuals. Kira just couldn't let go of the hope that she could somehow make things better. "By the way, I moved Betsy and Cody, so Mickey won't be able to find them."

"You moved them? Already?"

She nodded. "Today, with my parent's help. I don't know what evidence Mickey thinks they have, but if he found me, he would have found them. We've never had anything like this happen before. They're out of the country for now, and it's undocumented. Only my supervisor knows where they really are, besides me."

Dallas smiled, a puzzling expression on his face.

"What's that odd look for?" she asked, pulling her hand from his. She felt her heart beat faster when Dallas leaned close and touched his lips to her cheek.

"You're amazing," he said. "You just keep surprising me." He pulled her into his arms. For a long time, they held each other as if they'd known one another for years.

His shirt smelled like it had just come out of the laundry. The clean smell mingled with a slightly spicy aroma that was both soothing and invigorating. "Thank you for sharing that with me, Dallas. It does help to know that the feelings won't paralyze me forever."

"You have to make that choice," he said quietly. "It only has as much control as you give it."

Kira paused a moment, then let go of Dallas, easing away. "I have all of Cody and Betsy's records here. I've looked and looked, but I don't see anything that would be of interest to a drug dealer. Would you help me search through them and see if we can figure out what he's hunting for?"

"Sure, I'll clean off the table while you get the file," he said, standing. "Is it okay that you brought it home?"

"All's fair in love and war, and besides, I did it for Cody and Betsy's safety."

Dallas paused, glancing at her speculatively. "Kira…" He walked toward the kitchen and turned to her.

She cut him off before he could finish. "It's temporary, and my supervisor knows everything involved in my decision. She gave her stamp of approval on my idea. In the children's file at the office, the paperwork looks perfectly normal, except the house listed doesn't exist. Nor does the street it's on. I've totally removed the home they were in from the mock file. I don't want to endanger a good family."

He crossed his arms over his chest and furrowed his brow. "How many rules have you broken?"

"I stopped counting. Cody and Betsy have been through enough in their short lives," she said defensively, trying to ignore how strong and yet sympathetic Dallas was despite his attempts to sound tough. "I'm all they have now."

"You're—"

She held up a hand to silence him. The emotion of all of this was getting to her. "I'll be right back with the file. Let's focus on that." She raced upstairs to her room, where she'd hidden it.

Kira took a deep breath, collapsed against the closet door and closed her eyes. "God, please help Dallas and me to find Mickey and figure out what he wants, and soon. And if you have a chance, help Dallas see through his pain to let others in, especially someone who could love him the way he needs to be. I see how hard he's trying to make me believe he's a tough, cynical cop, but all I see is the compassionate man who would walk on broken glass to protect others. And if that someone isn't supposed to be me, would you take my rose-colored glasses off?"

Dallas had finished cleaning the kitchen in a matter of minutes, leaving him too much time to wonder what was taking Kira so long. He studied the framed collage of snapshots of her and her brothers. *What was it she said about the other brother who wouldn't be showing up?* Though some of the photos were from when they were young, he didn't see a fourth boy in any of them. Had one of them died? Or was it a brother from her birth family?

The Matthews' looked like a happy family, despite the fact that their father was a cop and they had an adopted sister. Other than the different skin color, one would never guess they weren't full siblings. Finger "bunny ears" and goofy smiles hadn't missed this family. While most brothers picked on sisters, the Matthews boys seemed protective of Kira, more than if she had been their natural sister.

He wondered if she planned on having a family. While she'd ended up in a happy home, she'd also mentioned running away from foster homes and having a mysterious brother that she apparently hadn't forgotten. Dallas's focus landed on a picture of Ted and Kira when she was very young. She had the biggest smile and a tight grip on her dad's neck.

"I see you found Mom's wall of memories," Kira said from behind him. She had an oversize manila envelope in her arms and motioned toward the sofa.

"It's a cool idea. I think I'll look for those frames for my mom's birthday. She'd love it, too." He didn't want to tell Kim how much it revealed about her family.

Dallas followed her to the table, where she was spreading out the contents of the envelope. Photos and phone messages spilled across the surface. "All this is from that night?" he said, as he pulled out a chair for Kira, then scooted one close to her for himself.

"Nope, their mom has been through this several times before. Which is why I'm going to proceed with a permanent placement for Betsy and Cody as soon as things settle down. Their mother's had several chances and can't stay clean for more than a few months. We didn't realize it until we entered her name in the state registry.

We immediately heard from Denver County Child Services, and they sent several more documents to help our cause."

Dallas looked at the photos of the night they'd taken the children from their Antelope Springs home, and even older pictures, when Betsy was in an infant carrier. "Don't get me wrong, they seem like okay kids, but surely you can't devote yourself this much to every child you work with. Why do these two mean so much to you?"

She was silent for a while. "Because…" She faltered, "Wow, I haven't consciously thought about it since that night, but remember when Cody told you he could take care of his sister?"

Kira looked into his eyes and waited.

Dallas tried to remember, but couldn't. "I'm sorry, I don't recall that. What happened?"

"You were carrying Betsy to the car for me. She was upset, and Cody took her from you and said he'd take care of her." Kira's voice was so soft, her gaze so distant, that Dallas had no doubt she was reliving every moment of that night. "Ever since then, I knew I had to keep them together at all costs. They remind me of my brother, who was taken away from me."

Dallas set the pictures on the pile and turned to face Kira, resting his elbow on the back of their chair.

"When my parents died, my stepdad's family took my brother, because he was a blood relative and they felt obligated."

Dallas nodded, fearing he knew the rest.

"They didn't want me because I'm not their family. Ted—Dad, I mean—was the officer who met with the social worker after the accident, and who had come to tell us we had to go into foster care. He watched them turn me away." Tears welled up in her eyes.

"Oh man, that's cruel." Dallas extended his arm and touched her shoulder. Immediately she snuggled against him, and he rested his cheek against her head.

"Dad promised he'd find a good home for me, and he did, but it took a long time to get through all of the paperwork and find all the loopholes. Cody and Betsy need each other. I can't let anything happen to them."

"I understand." Dallas loosened his arms and looked at her, thinking how blessed the two children were to have Kira in their corner.

A few minutes later, Dallas felt his phone vibrate, but he ignored it. He could call whoever it was back. Seconds later the doorbell rang, and Kira jumped.

Dallas pulled his phone off his belt. "Wait…" He looked at the phone, punching buttons. "My cell just rang." They both stood, and Dallas checked to see who was calling. "It's your brother, uh, Kent? Is he the narc?"

"Yeah," she said, glancing toward the foyer as she heard keys jangling against the door. "It must be Mom and Dad home already. Why is my brother—?"

Before Dallas could get past Kira, the door, swung open to reveal Kent standing there, a phone to his ear.

Get 2 Books FREE!

Steeple Hill Books, publisher of inspirational fiction, presents

Love Inspired
SUSPENSE

A SERIES OF EDGE-OF-YOUR-SEAT SUSPENSE NOVELS

FREE BOOKS!
Get two free books by acclaimed, inspirational authors!

FREE GIFTS!
Get two exciting surprise gifts absolutely free!

2 FREE BOOKS

▲ To get your 2 free books and 2 free gifts, affix this peel-off sticker to the reply card and mail it today!

We'd like to send you two free books to introduce you to the *Love Inspired*® *Suspense* series. Your two books have a combined cover price of $9.98 in the U.S. and $11.98 in Canada, but they are yours free! We'll even send you two wonderful surprise gifts. You can't lose!

Each of your **FREE** books is filled with riveting inspirational suspense featuring Christian characters facing challenges to their faith... and their lives!

GET 2 FREE BOOKS!

HURRY!
Return this card promptly to get **2 FREE Books** *and* **2 FREE Bonus Gifts!**

Love Inspired.
SUSPENSE

YES! *Please send me the 2 FREE Love Inspired® Suspense books and 2 FREE gifts for which I qualify. I understand that I am under no obligation to purchase anything further, as explained on the back of this card.*

affix free books sticker here

323 IDL EL4Z   123 IDL EL3Z

FIRST NAME	LAST NAME

ADDRESS

APT.#	CITY

STATE/PROV.	ZIP/POSTAL CODE

Steeple Hill®

Offer limited to one per household and not valid to current subscribers of Love Inspired® Suspense. **Your Privacy -** Steeple Hill Books is committed to protecting your privacy. Our Privacy Policy is available online at www.SteepleHill.com or upon request from the Steeple Hill Reader Service™ From time to time we make our lists of customers available to reputable firms who may have a product or service of interest to you. If you would prefer for us not to share your name and address, please check here ☐.

Steeple Hill Reader Service™—Here's How It Works:

Accepting your 2 free books and 2 free gifts places you under no obligation to buy anything. You may keep the books and gifts and return the shipping statement marked "cancel." If you do not cancel, about a month later we will send you 4 additional books and bill you just $3.99 each in the U.S. or $4.74 each in Canada, plus 25¢ shipping & handling per book and applicable taxes if any.* That's the complete price, and — compared to cover prices of $4.99 each in the U.S. and $5.99 each in Canada — it's quite a bargain! You may cancel at any time, but if you choose to continue, every month we'll send you 4 more books, which you may either purchase at the discount price...or return to us and cancel your subscription.

BUSINESS REPLY MAIL
FIRST-CLASS MAIL   PERMIT NO. 717-003   BUFFALO, NY

POSTAGE WILL BE PAID BY ADDRESSEE

STEEPLE HILL READER SERVICE
3010 WALDEN AVE
PO BOX 1867
BUFFALO NY 14240-9952

NO POSTAGE
NECESSARY
IF MAILED
IN THE
UNITED STATES

If offer card is missing write to: Steeple Hill Reader Service, 3010 Walden Ave., P.O. Box 1867, Buffalo, NY 14240-1867

"Hey, I was just calling you." He looked at Kira, then Dallas, and grinned sheepishly.

Dallas closed his phone and clipped it back to his belt. "Yeah, I recognized the number. What's up?"

"Where are Mom and Dad? Do they know you have company?" Kent asked with a suspicious look in his eyes.

Kira put her hand on her hip. "Don't even start with me, Kent. Why are you here? And why are you calling Dallas?"

"I figured you'd miss Mutt and Jeff grilling Dallas." Her shaggy-haired brother laughed. "I need you both to come with me. Mickey's in Denver."

"They have him in custody?" Kira felt the mood brighten.

Kent shook his head. "Well, sort of. He's dead."

TWELVE

Kira stacked all the papers into the file and put it back in the envelope. Before they left town, she ran up to her room and put it away. She might be a skeptic, but until she saw for herself, she wasn't going to believe that Mickey Zelanski was no longer a threat.

When she returned to the foyer, Kent was waiting for her. Dallas was nowhere in sight. "You really like him, don't you?" her brother asked.

"Shh!" Kira said, covering his mouth with her hand. "Where is he?"

Kent brushed her hand away. "He went out to his car. He offered to drive." Her brother was staring at her. "Man, you have it bad!"

"I do not!" she insisted, looking for her purse. "Did you call Dad?"

"He didn't answer, so I left him a message." Kent lifted her purse from behind the coat rack. "Here, is this what you're looking for?"

She groaned. "How do you do that?"

He shrugged. "I've been married for ten years, so I know how women think."

"Renee might argue with you about that," Kira said with a laugh.

"I beg to differ. Care to test me?"

She thought a minute about how to stump him. "Fine, go ahead."

He smiled. "You sure you want to go there, sis?"

"Sure. I'm in a good mood," Kira declared.

"Okay, but remember who asked for it." He touched his fingers to his forehead and closed his eyes. "You're thinking 'I like Dallas, and I don't care if my brothers don't.'"

She tried to hide her shock. "Not even close."

Kent laughed out loud. "Close enough, though. For the record, you've got good taste this time."

"Why, because he's a cop?"

"It definitely gives us something to talk about with this guy. Better than that astrophysicist. And it's clear Mutt and Jeff must approve, or they wouldn't razz Dallas. You know, it's a brother's duty to chase off the riffraff. But I think Dallas could be good for you."

"I don't think I asked for your approval," she said as she headed out the door. "And I don't need Mutt and Jeff's help chasing guys off, either. Too bad you weren't this concerned for the people involved with Mickey."

Kent let out a groan. "Oh come on, I know you don't

want to face reality, Kira, but Zelanski's only one of several dozen drug dealers that we're watching."

"Well, someone wasn't watching very closely. Those kids aren't easily missed."

"We didn't know that kids were connected in any way. You know me better than that. Whether you like it or not, Kira, sometimes the bad guys stay one step out of our reach."

She stopped, then turned to face him. "I'm sorry," she said as she hugged him. "It's just that I think you leap tall buildings in a single bound. So it's not easy finding out you're human. Not to mention it's been a lousy week." She held on tight before letting him go. "And as far as the other subject, cool it. Even if I am interested, he's not."

Kent closed and locked the door behind them. He chuckled. "We'll have to fix that."

"Oh no, you don't. If I want your help, I'll ask for it," she insisted. She'd been through a lot of emotional upheaval lately, and Dallas had been there for her. Despite telling her brothers that he wasn't interested in a relationship, she had a gut feeling that he was changing his mind about the matter. In the meantime, she was content getting to know more about him before they dated. She wanted a forever friend. A permanent relationship. That couldn't be found in a few weeks. Or could it? She had a lot to pray about tonight.

Two hours later, Kira, Dallas and her brother had finally made it through Denver traffic and police red tape and were staring at a sheet covering the suspected body of Mickey Zelanski, wondering who had killed him, and why.

"Let us know if this is the man you saw, Kira."

Her heart beat faster as the coroner started to pull back the sheet. She closed her eyes, remembering the face of the man trying to break into the cruiser. Surely it wouldn't be the same one. She felt a strong arm embrace her.

"Kira, it's okay. Your brother and I are here with you. Just take a quick look and it'll be over," Dallas said in a deep, comforting tone.

It was hard to breathe as she opened her eyes. She inhaled quickly, then instinctively held her breath, shock hitting her in the stomach. She nodded. "That's him."

Kent discussed the specifics with the local homicide detective as Kira tried not to embarrass herself by losing her dinner.

"You don't have to stay in here," Dallas told her, passing his palm to her back to help her out of the morgue.

"Any personal belongings on him?" she heard her brother ask as she rushed out the door, with Dallas on her heels, determined to keep up with her. Kira inhaled deeply, filling her lungs with the nonpungent oxygen. She paced the hallway, willing her brother to hurry.

"Nothing on his person," she heard the investigator say. "Death seems to be—"

Kira plugged her ears. Her stomach couldn't take much more tonight. She dragged in another deep breath.

Dallas patted her shoulder as she made another lap past him. "You need a soda or something?"

"No, thanks," she muttered, ignoring his attempt to comfort her. She didn't dare stop pacing, for fear she might collapse into his arms and never let go. Kira wanted tonight over with. She wanted to be alone. She wanted privacy so she could fall apart. She wanted to let go and cry. "I'm fine, if you need to go back in there," she said to Dallas, hoping he would take the hint. She didn't need a witness to her continued struggle.

"I can hear okay from here." He stayed next to the door, but kept an eye out for her. She felt like a child. She couldn't deny that it was nice to have his attention, even if it was getting old being the damsel in distress.

As she watched Dallas strain to keep up on the investigation, she wondered what he was like when he wasn't in police officer mode. What had brought him from Phoenix to rural Colorado? Antelope Springs wasn't exactly the center of the universe, but she'd grown up in the area, and called it home.

She glanced at Dallas, hoping he wasn't a mind reader. Feeling horribly guilty that her thoughts were nowhere near the case involving the dead man in the next room, she looked down the hall, in the opposite direction of Officer Dallas Brooks.

Suddenly, she realized she hadn't found out much about Dallas. What she did know was important, but she hadn't gotten to know him nearly well enough to explain these feelings. He might be heroic, but when the crisis was over, would he be content to spend his nights off watching a movie and eating popcorn? Joining a couples' Bible study? Did he believe in God on the surface, or was it a deep, lasting faith? She knew from her own family that faith had to come from within, as the duties of the job often kept police officers from attending church services. *God, I don't understand what all of this is about. Is it over now? Does that mean I won't see Dallas again? Why did you bring him into my life?*

Kira collapsed on the sofa in the waiting room. She heard the door open again, and watched Dallas go back into the examination room.

Dallas waited until Kira had stopped pacing and sat down in the waiting area before he returned to the morgue, where the investigator, medical examiner and Kent were discussing Mickey's death. Dallas asked to see what evidence they'd bagged from the crime scene.

The police investigator held up a clear bag. "His wallet was cleaned out and dumped at the end of the alley." Kent held it up to the light and examined it while the next piece of evidence was handed to Dallas. "We found this in the very bottom corner of the bill slot. Whoever cleaned him out was thorough. His driver's license and the wallet were several hundred feet away from each other. We're still trying to figure out why they left it behind."

Kent studied the scrap of paper through the plastic. He pulled out his cell phone and took a close-up photo of the numbers scribbled on the corner. "Whoever killed him wanted the body identified," he said without emotion. "It's my guess they're sending a message to their other dealers." He drew out the word *dealers* as if he'd thought of a new angle on the investigation. "Give us a few days before you release this to the press. I have a hunch I'd like to follow. And be sure to let me know what you find on the prints from the wallet."

"Sure thing," the investigator responded.

Kent signed some paperwork and they joined Kira.

"Do you know any of Zelanski's contacts?" Dallas asked Kent as they walked back to the car.

"Say, I'm starved. You two mind if we stop for a bite to eat?" he said instead of answering.

"No-o-o, thank you," Kira said, in as polite a tone as she could muster. "But you can get something if you want."

They pulled through a fast-food restaurant to get Kent supper on their way back to Fossil Creek.

"So anyway, we were working on Zelanski's dealers," Kent finally replied. "We were getting close, and then Zelanski disappeared off the radar. We'd catch a clue, follow the lead, and then he'd vanish again."

A few minutes later, Dallas merged onto the interstate. "Sounds like Zelanski made your informant." He tapped the steering wheel with his fingers as the Denver traffic came to a standstill.

"That's what we thought," Kent continued. "It had been quiet for a few weeks, then last weekend he was back in business...same cell number, but we couldn't ever find him. We're working with the Drug Enforcement Administration on the case."

"That was after we uncovered his supply, right?" Dallas asked. "Maybe he wasn't calling anyone because the meth hadn't arrived."

"Well," Kent said hesitantly, "we have another hunch about that, too, and this homicide fits right in with that suspicion. The newer shipments of meth coming through the region are higher quality, which is putting a real crimp in the market. The dealers are getting complaints from their users about the diluted stuff. They want the high grade meth."

"This wasn't a meth kitchen, right?" Kira looked to Dallas. "I mean, I didn't see any of the usual signs of a meth kitchen."

Kent interrupted. "New restrictions have put a crimp in the production of meth. This case we've been building brings the purest stuff in from labs along the Mexican border. They use Mexican nationals to bring the drugs into the United States. We're right on the interstate, so it's a direct route, and the nationals easily blend in with the population in the area."

Kira was beginning to follow their thinking. "But that doesn't explain why Mickey was after me. I don't have anything that would matter to him."

Kent picked up on another idea. "That's true, but you know where Betsy and Cody are, and who knows how much they know? Looks like we need to visit with Mickey's girlfriend and the children, see how this news hits them."

"It's also possible that Mickey was calling his mules to warn everyone that he'd be late on his delivery. He's on the run, trying to keep his supplier happy while he pulls together the cash…" Dallas was thinking out loud. "He's getting panicked that he can't get the dope to his runners, to get the cash. He doesn't want to tell anyone that the DEA has his merchandise."

"I think there's more to it than that. We had him connected to Raul Sorento drug kingpin of the Rockies. A few weeks ago, someone intercepted Raul's shipment as it left Nevada. I suspect you found the shipment. Mickey's edgy and Sorento's been a little cranky ever since. He's got his thugs running all over the place, trying to find his supply. This is the second death we can connect to him this week."

"Let's go talk to Cody as soon as we get to town," Dallas insisted.

"Wait a minute," Kira exclaimed. "It's almost ten, Dallas. By the time we get to the ranch it will be midnight. We can't barge in there now." She let out a loud yawn. "I can go get Cody and Betsy in the morning. Now that Mickey's gone, they need to be back in their own school."

Dallas turned his head momentarily, since she was in the back seat. "Did Cody ever tell you what started the fight between him and Mickey?"

"No."

"So where is he, exactly?"

"On our aunt and uncle's ranch on the Colorado-Nebraska," Kira announced. "Too far away to head out there now."

Kent vouched for the fact that they weren't going to see Cody tonight. "I can't imagine anyone who doesn't know the way finding the place, especially at night," he stated. "We know where it is, and *I've* gotten lost going out there."

"Tomorrow then, we need to talk to all of them."

"I know, I know. I'll get them back here."

Traffic on the interstate was slow moving, with frequent long stops due to overnight road construction. Even as midnight approached, there wasn't a break in the line of cars. Kira found herself dozing off, waking occasionally to hear Dallas and Kent in nonstop conversation. But despite her efforts, she couldn't stay awake.

She slept until Dallas pulled to a stop in front of her parents' house. Her brother helped her out of the car, and she realized what a disaster her evening with Dallas had been.

"Kira," Dallas said, leaning across the seat. "I'll call you tomorrow."

"Okay," she murmured, feeling more than a little disappointed about the way the evening had turned out, even though it wasn't ever intended to be a date. "Sorry we missed dessert."

"Save me a piece of that chocolate cake. Your brother told me it's worth the wait."

She smiled. "I hope he didn't say anything stupid while I was napping back there." Now she felt like a teenager. "Thank you again for coming tonight. I know how difficult it was to tell me about what happened."

"It was time I move on to the next step. Hey, thanks for a terrific dinner. I'd come in to thank your dad for picking out a great steak, but it's late and he's probably asleep by now. Next time I see him, I'll be sure to thank him myself." Dallas raised an eyebrow. "Just think, once all of this is settled, we can go out to dinner in a restaurant, like a normal couple."

Kira's heart skipped a beat. "Sounds good. Drive carefully going home, Dallas." She watched until his tail lights faded away. *Kent did say something stupid.*

She turned and ran into the house after her brother, coming to a sudden halt when she discovered her parents were still awake. "Hi," she said, feeling like a guilty adolescent. "Dallas thanked you for picking out a great steak, by the way." She smiled. Despite the emotional evening, she felt lighter than a cloud.

"Hi," her parents said in unison, sounding suspicious.

"So Mickey's really out of the way, huh?" her dad asked.

She hit the ground faster than a bolt of lightning. The smile faded from her heart as the reality of a cop's world returned. "Yep, he's history," she told them, unable to hide her relief.

"Kira," her mother scolded, "a man was just killed!"

Kira stared at her in disbelief. "I didn't mean that to sound so irreverent, but he did threaten me...."

Kent hid a smile. "Change the subject," he whispered from the side of his mouth.

Kira felt as if they were ten years old again, lined up for an inquisition as to who ate the dessert Mom had just prepared for a dinner party. "And you, mister, what did you say to Dallas while I was asleep?"

His mouth twitched, and she knew not to believe a word he was about to say. He shrugged. "I just reminded him that we have plenty of shotguns, in case he had thoughts of breaking your heart. He asked if we had plans for Memorial Day weekend, mentioned a huge cake and punch."

Kira rolled her eyes, and her parents' shock was almost worth the bad joke. "He's kidding."

"Better be," Dad grumbled. "I barely met him."

Her mom's eyes lit up. "I didn't even get a chance to talk to him. I thought this was some official meeting. It was a date?"

Kira took a deep breath and smiled. "No. It was business, but I wouldn't mind if he did ask me out on a real date. And back to business... Since Mickey's out of the picture now, we have more questions to ask the children. I'm going out to get the kids from the ranch in the morning, so I'd better get some sleep."

"Want me to drive you out there?" Kent offered.

"That poor car of yours would fall apart on the dirt roads. Thanks, anyway, I've had enough excitement for one week."

"I want to know what you find out," Kent hollered as she ran up the stairs.

"I'll think about it," she teased.

THIRTEEN

Dallas reported to school the next day, totally unprepared to be greeted by the flirtatious receptionist. "Hi, Officer Brooks."

He looked up from his desk, terrified to think what she was doing in his office. "Morning. What can I do for you?"

"I talked to the principal after you left yesterday. Once he heard there are problems with security, he changed his schedule, and he's available now. I left you a message at your house last night. Didn't you get it?"

He frowned, wondering how she'd gotten his unlisted number. "Tell Mr. Davidson I'll get my notes and be right there."

He hurried down the hall, tearing his mind from Kira and the Zelanski case. After barely five hours of sleep, he was already wishing that final bell would ring.

Last night hadn't gone at all as he'd hoped it would. He'd wanted to know more about how Kira was feeling. How she was coping with the anxiety. Now, thankfully,

Mickey was no longer a threat, but Dallas was too much of a realist to believe that whoever killed Zelanski wouldn't eventually come looking for the same things that Mickey had been after.

Dallas glanced at his watch. He had an hour, hopefully uninterrupted, before the first bell rang. He talked fast, explaining his concerns to the middle-aged principal. Issues related to school violence had changed in recent years, and Dallas was prepared for his concerns to be brushed aside by someone with more experience in schools than he had. Besides that, staff at smaller schools tended to think they were less likely to be affected than inner city schools. Recent history was proving that theory wrong, too.

Mr. Davidson leaned back in his chair and nodded. "I've tried to address these concerns at teacher meetings. Things get better for a week or two, and then everyone lets them slide again. Brad was strong with the students one-on-one, but he didn't like to crack down on anyone after he'd made friends. He seemed to think he knew the community well enough to realize if there were going to be issues. Can't count on that these days, either."

Dallas didn't want to share his experience with school violence, but neither did he want to repeat it. Not every school had an Alek in it, but with the increase in traumatic events, he wasn't going to take his chances. "Mr. Davidson, I don't want to discredit the way things have been done here before. Times have changed, and unfortunately, we need to be proactive in our approach. Even then, there's no guarantee." He opened the school's crisis manual, wondering how Mr. Davidson could ignore the facts. Tragedy could happen anywhere. All it needed was opportunity.

Principal Davidson shook his head. "We'll make the changes, but I want you to be prepared for an uphill battle. The parent accountability board had complaints about being inconvenienced when they come to volunteer or to attend parent-teacher conferences. I can't imagine how they'd feel if something did happen because they didn't want to walk a little farther. We all caved to the pressure. It wasn't any one person's fault. Common case of the squeaky wheel gets the grease."

"Glad to hear we're of the same opinion on that." Dallas had half the battle won. "We need to know who is in the building at all times, and feel confident that we can keep our eye on who's coming and going. The best way to do that is to use one entrance, but if that isn't possible, we need to make sure office and custodial staff, security cameras or teachers are monitoring everyone coming and going."

"This exit here has always been the biggest challenge," Davidson said, his finger on a blueprint of the school.

Within the hour, they had evaluated the layout of the building and agreed to direct all students to use just two doors during the school day. Traffic from the six outbuildings would have to funnel to those same two doors, south and west.

As the bell rang, the principal was adding the change to the announcement list. He said he'd watch and make sure someone was assigned to each door, to remind students to use the proper exits and not let anyone in through emergency exits. Signs were made and posted.

Dallas felt positive about the changes and wondered if it was more than a coincidence that he had found a job in Antelope Springs. God certainly had been pushing him to get back into law enforcement somehow. The security positions he'd considered after his treatment would have been a huge mistake. He realized that now. There was no way he could have settled for calling in the police and standing down until they could take over.

He stood near the main entrance, ignoring the faces as students walked past. The kid who liked to work in Brad Johnson's office stopped and waved his hand in front of Dallas's face, like tourists did to the guards at Buckingham Palace.

"Hey, Brooks, how's it going?"

Dallas froze. He thought he'd made it clear the day before that he wasn't here to be buds.

"Earth to cop," the youth said with a goofy grin that looked something like a Jim Carey impression.

This wasn't a prison, Dallas realized. "Morning, Tucker." *It wouldn't kill me to lighten up a little,* he thought. "How're you today?"

The teenager shrugged. "Not bad. Homework is

done—" he waved his spiral notebook in the air "—and the tardy bell hasn't rung yet."

Dallas felt his lips twitch and a chuckle escape. He glanced up at the clock. "With thirty seconds to spare, even."

Tucker took off running. "Later, Brooks!"

Dallas shook his head as the clusters of teenagers disbursed instantly, seconds before the bell rang.

By lunchtime he'd received two complaints from parents about the locked doors, resulting most likely from the stack of tardy slips the reinforced policy had generated. Dallas noticed an additional half-dozen commendations from teachers and other staff. Not bad for the first day, he thought. Next week he'd plan a lockdown drill. Just because the year was almost over didn't mean they were out of the woods. It was no time to get lax on safety.

As he turned to go back into his office to return phone calls, he saw Kira and Cody walk through the front doors.

"Afternoon," Dallas said to them both, noticing that Cody appeared to have gained ten pounds, and looked great. Kira looked as tired as Dallas felt. "I kind of thought you'd call," he told her.

She gave him a half hearted smile and shook her head. "I was going to wait until after school, but we got away earlier than we expected and here we are." She was obviously tense after the drive. As many times as she'd had to move Cody and Betsy from home to home, doing so was no doubt getting old.

Dallas tried to read what the kid was thinking and what Kira had told him. "Let's go into my office," he murmured. As they walked down the hall to the small room that held his desk, a file cabinet and a couple of chairs, Dallas made an effort to break the ice. "Hi, Cody, how is it going?"

"What are we doing here? I thought we weren't coming back to Antelope Springs. Officer Brooks, tell Miss Matthews that me and Betsy need to get away from this town. It ain't nothing but trouble for us. We don't even have our own things here anymore. And Mickey's going to find us for sure if we're back here."

Dallas looked at Kira, trying to hide his shock. "Sit down, Cody. Miss Matthews, here's a chair for you." He closed the door and leaned against the desk.

"Cody," Kira said, "I'm sorry I couldn't explain everything to you without Officer Brooks present. We're working together to figure where might be the best and safest place for you."

Cody jumped to his feet. "You're sending me to juvie?"

"What?" Kira dropped her bag and held out her arm to block the doorway. "No. No!" She apologized for her bad choice of words. "We're going to find a good, permanent home for you and Betsy. Honest. I know what you are going through, and I'm not going to separate you two. I promise."

"Yeah, right. Heard that before. It's been two houses already, probably a third tonight, right?" He looked around the tiny office, his gaze landing on Dallas. "What're you doing in Officer Johnson's office?"

"He needed some time off. I'm filling in."

That seemed to settle okay with the kid. Kira sat down again and motioned for Cody to do the same.

Then she leaned forward, resting her elbows on her knees. "Cody, Officer Brooks and I need to talk to you a little more about what happened the night we were called to your house."

"How come? Did something else happen?"

Kira looked at Dallas, silently asking him to do the honors. *No use wasting time here.* Dallas crossed his arms over his chest. "Yes, something more has happened, Cody. First I want you to tell me about your relationship with Mickey, before that night."

Cody eyed Kira, who had a strained look on her face. "Betsy and I don't like him."

Dallas waited a minute, hoping the boy would go into more detail. "Can you tell me why?"

He squirmed in his chair, holding tight to his backpack. Finally he shrugged. "I dunno. Why? What'd he tell you?"

"Nothing. We haven't talked to Mickey," Dallas said. "Did you and he fight a lot?"

"Yeah, kind of, I guess." Cody glanced at Kira and his eyes got huge. "You're not going to send us back with him, are you?"

Kira was caught off guard. "No," she said, shaking her head. "Never." Then she added, "And you know that your mother isn't going to be able to come home, either, don't you? I don't want you to have a false expectation."

"Yeah, I know. She's an idiot to have gotten mixed up in drugs again." Cody said it with such seriousness that Dallas lost his edge. "But I'm going to take care of Betsy. I'm all she has left now. She misses Mom."

"Of course she does," Kira said sympathetically. "And I know that you feel responsible for taking care of Betsy, but that isn't…that isn't your responsibility."

Dallas understood. She had probably wanted to be there for her brother, and never forgave herself. She wasn't about to let Cody live with the same guilt. This case hit too close to home, just like returning to a school setting did for Dallas.

"Cody, we need you to help us figure out why Mickey was trying to find Miss Matthews. Do you have any ideas why he might have wanted to find her?"

Kira was still trying to regain her composure, and Cody frowned. "Did he beat you up, too?"

She shook her head. "No," she said hesitantly. "Did he beat you up?"

"Nah, but he did my mom." Cody looked at his backpack. "I don't think he really liked her. He's just using her and our house to hide his business."

"What makes you say that?"

Cody shrugged. "He never really talked nice to her. He made her run errands for him all the time. You know, meet his clients for him."

Dallas tried to ignore the insults popping into his head. "Did Mickey ever meet with his customers?"

He shrugged. "Not as much as Mom did. Sometimes, if she had to run a package when she was dropping us off at school, we'd go along. But don't tell Mickey. He don't know we found his stuff."

"Stuff?" Dallas said innocently.

"You know what I'm talking about, or we wouldn't be in foster care. I'm a kid, but I'm not stupid."

"Mickey can't hurt anyone anymore, Cody. But we need to find out who he was working with. We're hoping you can help us with that information."

Cody looked at Kira, then back to Dallas. "You caught Mickey?"

Dallas shook his head, watching Cody's expression as he broke the news. "Someone killed him yesterday."

Fear filled his eyes. "Really? You aren't pulling my leg, are you?"

"We won't lie to you," Dallas promised, watching as Cody tried to hide his tears. "Miss Matthews and I need to know why you were fighting with Mickey. What started the argument?"

The boy wiped his eyes. "Mickey was always mad when a new shipment came in. This time was even worse." Cody sobbed harder the more he fought for control. Kira started to comfort him, and Dallas held her back. Finally, Cody regained control. "I just wanted him to get out of our lives. He was a bully."

Kira nodded, but then she noticed Dallas looking at her, and she stopped. She switched mode, from sympathetic to the tough woman he needed to see right now. "We want to make sure everyone is safe now, Cody, and somehow, things just don't seem to be adding up."

The teen shrugged.

Dallas was out of ideas. Cody was holding back. Until he trusted them, they were out of luck. "Miss Matthews. Why don't you check him into classes and—"

"I don't want go to school here," he insisted.

"From what I understand, you didn't like it in Fossil Creek, either," Dallas said. "At least you know everyone here. You can pick up on your classes again. You know the teachers, and they'll work with you to get caught up. You've only missed a couple of weeks."

Kira agreed. "You only have four more weeks of school, Cody. Mickey's not a threat to you anymore, so we really have no reason not to bring you back home, do we?" She paused. "Okay then, your new foster home will be ready for you after school. I'll be back to meet you out front."

Cody sulked.

She stood and motioned for him to lead her to the office. "Officer Brooks will be here if you have problems."

The instant the words were out, she froze, as if she realized what she'd said. She stood and rolled the chair back to Dallas, mouthing a silent apology. Much as he wanted to ignore that this was part of his responsibility now, truancy, teenagers and their safety all went with the oath he'd taken to serve and protect. "You know where I am if you need something, Cody."

"I shouldn't even be in this school, and you know it."

Dallas recognized the attitude, and wasn't about to let him lay any guilt on him or Kira. "Unless you have other information for us, we have no reason to believe you're not safe here. So why do you think otherwise?"

Cody jumped up, opened the door and ran out of the office.

Kira stared at Dallas. "I'm sorry."

"Don't get too involved, Kira. You're going to get hurt." He watched as she joined Cody and the two of them walked down the hall. Dallas had the distinct impression he'd just been conned into mentoring another teenager.

Closing the door, he wondered how in the world he'd gotten back here, into the same situation he'd been in four years ago. "This wasn't in the message I heard, God. Not the school, and especially not the woman."

He dropped into his chair and opened his computer. looked at his watch and noticed that he had several minutes before the fifth-hour bell would ring. He picked up the phone to check on Cody's enrollment status. He didn't especially want to run into Kira again. She had enough to deal with right now.

"He just enrolled," the secretary said. "Mr. Davidson took him and the social worker to the classroom. You have some messages here."

"Thanks, Miss Carson. I'll come get them in a while."

Two hours to go until the day was over. A few minutes after sixth period started, he heard a soft knock on the door. He looked up from his e-mails and leaned back in the chair, motioning Kira inside.

"Cody settled?"

"He's here physically, but he definitely doesn't want to be." They talked for a few minutes about the case before Dallas realized that wasn't her reason for being here.

She took another tentative step.

"Have a seat," he suggested.

She leaned against the corner of his desk and folded her hands in front of her. "I'm so sorry about what I said, Dallas. It just slipped out." Kira fumbled with her words, and he found himself happy to see her again. "I don't want you to worry. I've told the school, and Cody, to call me if he needs anything. He won't bother you."

"I worry about you, Kira. And I don't think there's anything you can do to prevent it." Dallas felt his resolve weaken for the second time today. Much as he wanted to lock himself away from getting involved with others, he couldn't stop it.

"Why are you smiling?"

He raised his eyebrow. "I don't even know for sure. It's been a week of constant affirmation that as much as I want control over my life, and to close people out…" He felt the weight lift off his heart as he spoke. "God sends the most unlikely people to remind me that I need to forget what's behind me, and reach for what lies ahead. Or maybe in this case, reach out to the woman in front of me."

Though he longed to hold Kira, he crossed his arms over his chest, the protective bulletproof vest reminding him of the reality of his job. As impenetrable as the vest was, God's healing had gone right through it, he realized. Dallas couldn't shield himself from the Lord, or his purpose. And despite that realization, Dallas still struggled with handing all of the control to him. He'd worked too hard to get back on the job, back behind the badge, back in control. He knew his healing was God's plan, but he didn't like feeling as if God was his crutch. His faith had gotten him through the worst time in his life and enabled him to handle it. He couldn't let go this easily.

"I guess that answers one question I wanted to ask you," Kira said quietly, pulling his attention back to her.

A thoughtful smile curved her mouth and sent his pulse racing. "Yeah? And what was that?" As she spoke, he realized that the only way to keep from hurting those he cared about was to keep them at a distance. That meant Kira, too.

"If you've let God into your heart," she said softly. "If you've turned your life over to Him, the healing will come in His timing. I'm glad you've already started that process. Thank you for showing me that I can't separate myself from others because of a painful past."

Dallas felt the bars of his emotional prison slam shut.

He couldn't stand the thought of Kira being hurt. Even though he wouldn't mean to, it was bound to happen. She was a strong woman who had been through a lot in her life. With the shadows she already dealt with, she didn't need more. She didn't need his piled on top.

Suddenly, she turned toward the door, and Dallas realized they weren't alone. Kira reached into her bag, pulled out a business card and scratched a number on the back. "Call me after work and we can set a time to talk to Cody's sister," she said, so smoothly he wondered if the intimate discussion they'd just had was only in his mind.

Kira turned to leave, but was unable to get past the fuming receptionist.

Miss Carson held out a handful of messages, flicking them at Dallas before he took hold of them. "These are parents who want an explanation on the locked door policy. The superintendent's wife is one of them," she snapped, then turned and left.

He looked around the tiny office and back to Kira. They shared a sympathetic smile. Kira whispered, "One suggestion, Officer Brooks. Office romances are a really bad idea."

"Thanks," he said, "I'll keep that in mind, Miss Matthews."

Apparently the flying sparks weren't just in his imagination. *Great. Just when I thought things were looking up.*

FOURTEEN

After a talk with Betsy, an unproductive one, Dallas and Kira went to the county jail to talk to Shirley Mason, who'd just been transferred over from the drug rehab center. As part of the county-wide drug task force, Kent met them there. His connections to the DEA had been invaluable thus far, and they couldn't afford to burn any bridges now.

Dallas broke the news that Mickey had been killed.

Shirley shook her head, muttering swear words as tears streamed down her face. She looked like a zombie, and open sores spotted her face from years of meth abuse.

"In recent weeks, Mickey Zelanski vandalized a police car, left you to face drug trafficking charges, broke into Miss Matthews's home and threatened your son and daughter, ma'am. I don't think it's because he wanted to raise your children. What was he after?"

The string of profanity continued while the mother cried. "He and Cody had that fight. Cody was just trying to protect us. He begged me to help him find Mickey's drug money and run away."

Dallas nodded. "Do you have any idea where he kept the money?"

She mumbled something, but Dallas couldn't make it out.

"In a safe somewhere?" Kent asked. He wrote down the numbers that they'd found in Mickey's wallet and pushed the sheet of paper across the table. "These mean anything to you?"

Shirley jumped, as if she'd not seen Kent earlier. Her eyelids drooped, despite her surprise.

Kira sat next to her brother, hoping her presence would help ease Shirley's nerves. Shaking, the woman picked up the piece of paper and studied it, moving her lips in silence.

"Shirley, do you know what the numbers might refer to?" Kira pressed.

She started scratching a rash on her arm. "He'd just gotten a new cell phone, some berry thing, a few weeks ago. After this unexpected shipment came in."

"We haven't seen any cell phone. Do you know where it might be?" Kent asked.

Shirley looked at the table. "He insisted Cody took it, but he's a good boy. He wouldn't take something like that."

"Are you sure this isn't some part of his phone number?"

She looked at it again. "I don't think so, but…" She started reciting numbers to herself.

Kira leaned closer so she could hear to write them down.

Shirley shook her head. "Maybe it is. I just can't remember. It's not like I've been calling him lately." She began sobbing again. "He hasn't even sent me any lawyer."

"How did you reach him?" Dallas asked.

"Called him from my cell phone," she said cynically.

Dallas perked up. "Where is that?"

"Well, I don't happen to have it with me. I'm sure it was confiscated by your friends at the DEA when they arrested me." She was obviously becoming fed up with the questioning.

"Shirley, Cody feels very responsible for his sister, and it's clear that he was trying to help get you away from Mickey and the drugs. Do you think it's possible that he thought something on the phone could help you get away from Mickey?"

Shirley burst into tears again, and this time it took several minutes for her to calm down. "He's not a bad kid. He just don't know when to keep out of my business." She rambled on about wanting Cody to stay out of trouble and find a good life. Her twitch was getting worse.

Kira sympathized with the mother, but it was clear they weren't getting anywhere. "He was trying to help get you out of trouble, Shirley. And we want to make sure no one hurts him, or Betsy."

Dallas and Kent eyed one another. Shirley wasn't expecting them to push harder, so that's exactly what Kent did. "We need the names of Mickey's supplier and his dealers, Shirley. If you don't have them, where can we find them?"

Shirley's eyes opened wide and she began scratching her arm again, this time drawing blood. Kira pulled a tissue from her bag and handed it to her. She wondered how Shirley had managed to keep up with the day-to-day needs of her family.

The woman must have finally realized she was the only person left to keep her kids safe. "My life's already ruined, they told me." She spilled her guts. "He pays someone named Sorento. They'd just moved Mickey up in the operation, which doubled his take. We was trying to get it all out to the dealers that weekend. I don't know where to reach anyone now. Mickey said his old phone was broken, so he bought one of those fancy things where he can do e-mail, the Web, and find where he's going if he's lost. He'd just enter an address and it would tell him how to get there." She shrugged her shoulders. "I can't believe he needed all that fancy stuff. He was always messin' with the thing. Between that phone and refurbishing that dumb old RV, he wasted more money on toys…"

"What did the phone look like?" Dallas asked, making a mental note to come back to the recreational vehicle. Sounded like a good way to move drugs, and maybe a place to hide money.

"I dunno…." She shrugged again. "Rectangular, kinda like one of those old Game Boy things, only thinner and black. It's no wonder the kids thought it was a game. The fight that night was over a lousy phone!" Shirley dropped her head into her hands. When Dallas asked where Mickey kept the RV, and what it looked like, she said, "It was some old silver thing. Supposed to be worth something when he got done. He kept saying we'd move to a big, pretty house one day, too." She called Mickey a string of bad names and looked up to Kira. "Don't ever get mixed up with men," she said seriously. "They're nothin' but trouble. Look where it got me…."

"Shirley, if you think of anything else that might help us keep the children safe, let us know," she said soberly.

"Don't hold your breath. I don't have any idea where Mickey hid any of his stuff, I swear. I just want you to find it and get the…" She looked up at Kira and changed what she was going to say. "Catch that killer, before he kills my kids. Please!"

"What now?" Kira asked as they left the jail. "We don't know a great deal more than we did before."

"If Mickey had bought a new phone, there's a record of it somewhere, and if it's brand-new, it has a GPS chip. That means we can track it," Dallas said, "if we can find out the number."

"I'll get a warrant for the major cell phone companies to search their records. If we're up against Sorento and his thugs, we need to get answers quick," Kent stated as they reached the parking lot. "We need more information about that RV, too. And it's interesting that she mentioned the shipment arrived early. I'd lay odds Mickey's the one who took that shipment out from under Sorento."

"I'll keep a close eye on Cody at school, but I think it's wise to give him some space, see if he won't lead us to the phone, and maybe even the money, or the killer," Dallas said. "Or all three. Kira, can you let the foster family know we're looking for a cell phone or electronic device? Maybe he'd leave it at home while he's at school."

Kira shook her head. "The way he was clutching that backpack the other day, my bet is the phone is in there."

"When you brought him back from the ranch he had to bring all of his belongings, so it most likely was in the backpack then," Dallas mused. "But I don't think he'd take the chance of having something that valuable at school, where it would be much more easily stolen. That said, he's a teenager, and sooner or later, he's going to slip up."

Kira waited until Dallas confirmed that Cody was in school the next morning before she made an impromptu visit to the foster home. She hated to bring another problem case to the Woods, but they needed to know what was going on. Glen and Deb ran one of the county's best foster homes. It was a perfect place for kids like Cody and Betsy, who needed extra attention. Kira didn't expect the couple would turn the kids away, but she didn't want them to be caught off guard, by Cody or anyone else.

She explained the situation, and Deb helped her look, but unfortunately, their search of the siblings' belongings came up empty. Though Deb didn't recall seeing either of her charges playing with anything that looked like a Blackberry, she agreed to keep her eyes open and let Kira know if she found anything.

After working long days, Kira was almost caught up with her caseload again. She had several conversations with Dallas, on duty and off. He assured her that Cody was arriving on the bus each day and making it into school, but he continued to struggle to make it to class on time. By the end of the first week, he had already tallied half a dozen truancies, which gave her a perfect reason to stop at the school to chat with Dallas in person. He wasn't in his office, but she was able to track him down. "Good afternoon."

He spun around, seeming irritated to see her. "Hi," he said, giving her a quick once-over, as if unable to stop himself. Then he looked down the hall. "What brings you all the way out here?" He took off walking, beckoning for her to come along.

"I want to know if you've asked Cody why he keeps being tardy for his classes."

"You could have called to ask that."

Dallas's response startled her. "Is there something else I should know about?"

He remained silent as he marched to the main hall and then his office. "We can talk a little more freely in here." He stopped and waited for her to go in first, then closed the door before answering her question. "Cody avoids me, which works fine, since I can't really become the boy's shadow without raising too much suspicion."

"This is one way our agencies need to work closer together, Dallas. We're understaffed, and you're with him every weekday. I trusted you to let me know how he's doing here." Kira went on about his obligation to keep her informed about kids in the system.

"Fine, pull rank then. Just remember, we have rules that we need to follow, too, and you're stomping all over most of them. You've got to step back and let us do the investigating on the drug issues, Kira."

She rejected such an absurd idea. Her, breaking police policies? He was out of line. "My brother included me—"

"But he agrees with me," Dallas interrupted. "We needed you to identify Mickey. Yes, your role is important, we're not arguing that. But we don't want you hurt. And this is a dangerous case."

With a pulse-pounding certainty, she knew he wouldn't back down. He had at least one of her brothers on his side. Probably all of them, from the sound of it.

Kira gave a disgusted grunt. "So how is Cody adjusting?" she asked curtly.

Dallas was equally stubborn. "He's pushing a few buttons with his teachers, but overall he's toeing the line. I notice he's been walking around outside during lunch. Occasionally he leaves campus, which is not against the rules, so I can't stop him. "

"You can't follow him?"

Dallas slapped his chest. "I'm a little hard to disguise, even if I had time to follow one kid around."

"Why didn't you call me so *I* could follow him?"

"Because I had another critical issue to handle," he said in exasperation. "Cody's getting back into a routine, Kira. That's what we want him to do. He needs to get the impression that we trust him. And I need to know you trust me to do my job."

"Of course I do, but…"

"But? If you don't trust me to handle it, there are other options. If you want him watched 24–7, he needs to be somewhere else." Dallas pointed to the door. "I have a responsibility for all of the students here at the school— keeping boys from lighting girls' hair on fire, dealing with teenage drug dealers who are carrying more money in their backpacks than I earn in a month…"

As he continued to share the frustrations of his few weeks at the school, Kira's mind drifted back to the phone message she'd received the previous day from Family Finders, closing her search for Jimmie Driscoe, her brother. They'd found him, serving a ten-year sentence in a California prison for dealing large quantities of drugs.

"Maybe you're right, Dallas. But it could be that Cody just needs to know someone cares if he ruins his life." She walked out of Dallas's office and went directly to the main office to check Cody's attendance record and write down his schedule. If Dallas wasn't going to keep an eye on him, she would.

FIFTEEN

The following week, Kira rearranged her schedule so that she could visit Antelope Springs every day at lunch-time. She just hoped Dallas didn't find out. She parked close the first day so she could spot Cody coming out of school. The next day, she traded cars with her dad, and parked a little farther away, so she could stay out of sight.

Her heart broke as she watched Cody wander the campus alone. Where were his friends? Finally, the third day, Cody left the school grounds and began running. Starting the engine, she frantically tried to follow. Somehow, as she weaved her way through the housing development, she managed to, ending up at the elementary school. That must be where Cody had been going, she realized.

Kira saw him offer Betsy a bag of potato chips from his lunch, and the two shared the small treat. Then he pulled something from his pocket and took off again, back toward the high school.

The next two days, it was the same routine.

Though Kira had a terrible feeling Cody was creating trouble, she was relieved that he was going to the elementary school to check on Betsy.

The next Monday, she headed out to Antelope Springs High School yet again. She opened her car windows and pulled her lunch from its bag, ready to start up the motor as soon as Cody took off. She took a bite of her Asian chicken salad, struggling to see the almonds through the dark glasses she was wearing.

How she wished she and Jimmie had known where one another was when they were growing up. Maybe her brother wouldn't have rebelled so violently if she'd been there to check on him, she reflected. Had he been loved by his family, as she had been by the Matthewses? Or had he been raised in a dysfunctional family like Cody's? Did Jimmie feel the same sense of abandonment that she did each New Year's Eve, when she thought of her parent's hit-and-run accident? Did he even remember that night?

She pushed her floppy straw hat—today's disguise— out of her eyes, startled to see Dallas peering in the side window. She jumped, tossing salad all over herself.

Dallas's tight expression turned into an affectionately boyish smile as she opened the window. She plucked lettuce and mandarin oranges from her slacks. "Good thing I didn't have dressing on my salad!"

"Sorry about that. I've noticed you out here the last few days, wondered if there was a problem."

Kira didn't like the way her heart beat faster when he showed up. It seemed unfair that Dallas hadn't a clue how she felt about him. "Don't be a smart aleck, Dallas. Get in here before Cody sees you."

His laughter died as he crawled into the passenger's seat. "What do you think you're doing, spying on the kid in a getup like that?" He eyed the hat and smiled.

"You know why I'm out here," she said, determined not to let him soften her up. "You've barely told me a thing about Cody, so I'm here to watch him myself."

Dallas nodded somberly. "So you've figured out that he's going to the primary school to check on Betsy."

"You knew?"

He nodded again, seeming very sure of himself. "Of course."

"Then why didn't you tell me?"

"Because I want you to stay out of it and leave the police issues to the police. You make sure things are going well at the foster home. I'm able to handle the school side of it." The humor disappeared from his expression.

"What police issues? Is Cody in trouble?" She put the lid on her salad and removed her sunglasses.

"Kira, why won't you just trust me to handle it? I don't want you involved." Sweat beaded on Dallas's upper lip. His gaze darted down the block to the school grounds, then back to her.

"Yeah, well, like it or not, Dallas, I'm already involved."

"Too involved for your own safety. I thought I made

that clear last week. Why don't you trust me to do my job?" He waited, but she remained silent. "Do you have any idea how difficult it is to lose your heart to a woman who won't let you protect her?"

She didn't know what to say. She felt tears sting her eyes, and hurried to put the sunglasses on again. "I…you…" she said, and then her voice cracked.

"I was kind of hoping there'd be one more word in there." He pulled her sunglasses off and leaned across the console between them.

Kira looked away, afraid of getting lost in those warm, intense eyes. She had come here with her own agenda. And as usual, he was throwing a kink in it.

Her heart raced and her pulse pounded. She knew how difficult it was for Dallas to let anyone into his personal life. She wasn't about to admit she'd been in love with him since the first night they met. Not until he gave her more to go on than he was "losing his heart." *What does that mean, anyway?* "So…" she said breathlessly. "I don't see what that has to do with me."

"You don't?" He sounded truly confused.

They exchanged polite smiles and he leaned closer. "I'm falling in love with you, Kira."

"It's okay, I'll catch you," she whispered. "Trust me."

"I'm trying." His laugh was soft and strained. "You don't make this easy. I want you to go home and let me call you later."

"No." She crossed her arms. "Something always

comes up. I'm still waiting for a real date as a real couple, maybe even at a real restaurant. You should have figured out by now that you can't scare me away with platitudes, such as you're a cop and you have PTSD. I have baggage to pack up and put behind me, too. I'm ready to look ahead."

"You deserve better."

"I know what a cop's family life is like, Dallas. You don't walk out on the moments that matter, and you darn well better make the best of every minute together, good or bad. I'm not leaving until you tell me what's really wrong."

Dallas took her hand, and she held on tight, ignoring the fact that she wanted to know what his kisses would be like. *God, let me be here to catch him, today and forever*.

He drew a deep breath. "I've suspected the last few days that something is going on, someone's dealing, but I couldn't prove anything. Kids had these wads of bills, but no goods to be found. Their parents claim they want them to have money for an emergency, but they never even asked how much I'd found. I checked the parents out, and there was no known record of drug use. So today we found a girl collapsed in the bathroom. She'd eaten some Pop Rocks candy. It looked like candy. Smelled like strawberries. According to the EMT, her symptoms are classic for an overdose of meth."

Kira felt tears well up in her eyes again. "Is she okay?"

"We don't know yet."

"Is Cody involved?"

Dallas shook his head. "I hope not, but I'm hearing rumblings. I don't want to worry about you being caught in the middle of this again, Kira. If Cody is involved, *he* may need you to catch him." Dallas gave her a quick kiss and got out of the car.

She waited for him to walk across the street, but he ducked his head in the passenger-side window. "Can I pick you up for dinner at seven?"

"I'll be ready. Come to my place."

Kira put her glasses back on and started the car, her hands trembling. She considered going to the Woods' home, just in case something did happen, but realized that it would be worse to worry the couple if it didn't involve Cody. If something did happen, they'd handle it then. If it wasn't him, she'd hang a shadow of doubt over him that wouldn't be easy to get rid of.

Traffic seemed especially heavy between Antelope Springs and Fossil Creek today, which was extra annoying with someone tailgating her most of the way. Kira drove to the office and tried to focus on her job, but the minutes seemed to drag. She had the radio on, waiting for any word of the girls who'd overdosed, and thankfully, there was no announcement. Kira finally went home, hoping Dallas would call on his way to pick her up for dinner.

He arrived at ten to seven. She was ready to leave, but he stepped into the condo and quickly looked around. "You've been busy. It looks nice, definitely more like what I expected from you."

"You expected a neat freak?" she teased. "You've been talking to my brothers."

One corner of Dallas's mouth turned up in an irresistible smile. "Yes I have, but no, I figured that out all on my own."

Kira felt defenseless as she gazed into his blue eyes. *I can't believe he's really here*. She hoped tonight would finally be a normal date.

"Are we just going to stand here staring at each other?" she asked at last. "Not that I mind. You look great in uniform, but you look even better in your street clothes." His sand-colored slacks had actually been pressed, and his red button-down shirt looked brand-new.

He took a step closer and rested his hands on her shoulders, holding her at arm's length. "I think that's a perfect idea—staring at you. Life hasn't slowed down enough that we've had much of a chance to really be alone, and part of me would almost like to order takeout and hole up here. But a promise is a promise, and a real date it will be." He raised her chin and paused, thoughtfully studying her face. "You are a beautiful woman, Kira." Before she could respond, his lips brushed hers.

Kira felt her shoulders relax as he pulled her close, tenderly cradling her against him. As soon as he broke the kiss, she leaned close again, not wanting the magical moment to end.

A few minutes later, she pushed herself away from him. "I suppose we'd better pick a restaurant, before they stop serving."

Glancing at his watch, he smiled. "Where does the time go?"

She turned out the lights and grabbed her purse. They walked arm in arm to Dallas's car, outside the gate.

"You could have come on inside. There's a buzzer so you can call in from the gate."

"I needed the walk to settle my nerves," he said with a chuckle. "So what do you feel like eating tonight?"

Kira looked up as they crossed the street, startled to see a dark gray car parked on the next block. Was that the same car that had tailed her into town earlier?

She shook her head. She was definitely too involved when she started noticing ordinary cars and imagining them following her. As she and Dallas walked past, she tried to get a look inside, but the windows were tinted and she couldn't see a thing. "So, tell me," she said cautiously. "Do you wear your gun when off duty?"

Dallas tensed. "Where did that question come from?"

She shrugged, trying to tame her inner fears. If she told him about the car, they'd be back in her condo so fast she wouldn't know what day it was. They needed a night to be normal. She'd seen the worry that going out in public with the family placed on her dad and mom when he was on the force. Her dad was always concerned that someone he'd put away would retaliate against his family. That was even worse for Kent when he worked in narcotics. She wasn't going to do that to her and Dallas. "I'm just curious. My brothers say most cops wear their guns all the time. Well, except at home, I suppose."

"Is it going to upset you?"

She hadn't expected him to question her. Still, she would feel a lot more comfortable knowing he had a weapon with him. "I'm fine if you do carry one."

"I do," he said curtly.

Kira heaved a sigh of relief.

"And now you owe me an explanation."

"There's this quaint restaurant in Lyons. They have the most decadent fried cheese. How does that sound?" she said cheerfully.

He looked into her eyes, but she could tell he'd scoped out their surroundings, too. "What am I watching for, Kira?"

She raised upon tiptoe and pretended to kiss him on the neck. "I think that gray car behind me followed me from the school this afternoon."

Dallas pulled her close. "Hurry to the car."

He pressed the unlock button and they rushed into the vehicle. Dallas gunned the engine and backed out, squealing his tires just like the teenage boy who lived next door to her parents. Kira struggled to get her seat belt on as Dallas turned several sharp corners.

"I'm sorry, I didn't think anything of it at first," she said breathlessly. "And then I realized it had the same snake hanging from the rearview mirror."

"If I'd had my vest on I would have contacted him, but with dark windows like that, I don't take too many chances." He was silent for a few minutes, focusing on his driving and watching to see if the car was still following them. "I should have let him tail us now, rather than spend the night worrying that whoever it is is breaking into your condo. I sure hope it's just a terrible coincidence."

Kira was already on the phone.

"Who are you calling?" he asked.

"Garrett, to see if he can patrol the block more tonight. This is our first date. I don't want to come home to another disaster. And I don't want to have to stay with my parents again." After she left a message for her brother, Kira closed her phone and turned to see if anyone was following them.

Dallas eyed her briefly. "So did the guy make any aggressive movements this afternoon?"

She thought back to the drive, about being upset about Dallas's news, and shook her head. "I just got the impression he or she wanted to get around me. Traffic seemed heavy, and I was already pushing the speed limit. Finally, I slowed down, but the car rode my fender the rest of the way into town. I went to work, and we have a secured lot. I didn't notice if anyone followed me home later."

Dallas slowed down and turned into the first parking lot he found. "This is absurd. We've got to find out who it is, and what he wants."

"What?" she said, horrified. "This is our date. Our first date. I'd like it not to be our last."

"Are you going to enjoy it, worrying about the silver car?"

Why is this happening to us, God? She leaned her head back against the seat and closed her eyes. "Take me home, Dallas."

"I'm just going to go back and get the plate number and have your brothers run it. We'll go from there."

"Given the time it would take to return to the restaurant, we may as well order a pizza and eat at my place. You can join me or go home, it's up to you."

They drove back in silence. Just her luck, their first date was ruined, and the car was gone.

SIXTEEN

For a few days Kira's life seemed rather boring, in a wonderful sort of way. She and Dallas talked on the phone every evening, and with her routine pretty much back on track, she began to feel more secure. She hadn't seen the silver car recently, which comforted her, yet left her slightly on edge, too.

Even though their first date had been a bust, they did arrange to go to church together. She couldn't wait. Despite the difficulty of actually finding quiet time together, they were getting to know each other.

An hour before Dallas arrived to pick her up for the service, Cody's foster mom called. "Kira, I'm sorry to bother you on a Sunday morning, but Cody's gone."

Kira was caught totally off guard. "Gone where?"

"I don't know. Glen's gone out on the motorcycle looking for him. I've called all of his friends, but no one has seen him. We had an early breakfast, did chores and were getting ready to go to church. He didn't want to go.

We sent him to his room to think about his options, and when we went to check on him a while later, he was gone."

"I'll get there as quickly as I can," Kim exclaimed. As she drove out to their farm, she called Dallas to let him know she'd have to miss church.

"I'm going to contact the DEA agent, see if they've had any luck getting through to that phone, or heard anything about Sorento," he told her.

Ten minutes later, he called back. "Pick me up on your way through town. They think they have a location on the phone this morning. Maybe we can spot him."

By the time she got to Dallas's house, the news had changed. "The phone has been turned off and they've lost the signal. When they picked it up, whoever it was was south of the Woods farm."

"So Cody does have the phone?" Kira smacked the steering wheel. "Why won't he tell us he has it?"

Dallas shrugged. "Maybe he doesn't. Maybe he was giving it to someone else. Let's head out there, and maybe we'll luck out and intercept him as he comes back to the house."

Kira had a hunch that Cody had sneaked out of the house to use, dispose of or try to figure out what to do with the phone. She stopped a few miles from the farm and dialed the Woods' number. "Deb, it's Kira. Any word yet?"

"Yes," she confirmed. "I was going to call you, but I can't talk right now."

Kira could hear Glen's voice in the background. He was obviously giving Cody a firm talking to.

"Do you want me to stop by?" Kira asked, careful to stick to a question that Deb could answer with a yes or no.

"No, we're all on our way in to church. I'll talk to you later, okay?"

"That's fine. Do you mind if we look around outside for the phone while you're gone?" Kira asked.

"Sure enough," Deb said. "We'd appreciate it."

Kira looked at Dallas and let out a deep breath of exasperation. "Deb gave us her blessing. Can you get any closer to where he was when he used that thing? I'm going to find that phone before it kills someone else."

Dallas raised his dark eyebrows. "This is a side of you I don't think I've seen before." He opened his cell phone and called the agency back. "Can you give us the nearest crossroads to where the phone was used?" He paused. "No, I don't have a global positioning anything. Just give me highways, streets or county roads." He jotted numbers on his hand, then closed his phone. "We're looking for County Roads 84 and 19."

She turned south at the intersection of 86 and 19 and stepped on the gas so they wouldn't happen upon Deb and Glen. They didn't need to give Cody any more reasons to run today.

Kira pulled to the shoulder of the road and shut off the car. They got out and looked at the empty field.

"There's a tree over there. Maybe he hid it underneath. Where's the Woods' house?" Dallas asked.

Kira pointed to the north. "Somewhere that direction. They're on County Road 86. I think their address is 18-something or in the 18,000's, which means…" She turned and pointed toward the Rockies. "Numbers get larger as you go toward the mountains, so if this is County Road 19, they are east of here."

"Two miles," Dallas muttered. "May as well get started."

Twenty minutes later, Kira and Dallas had searched every possible hiding spot within a half mile of the car and found nothing more than a plastic container filled with trinkets and notes, under an abandoned tractor.

They looked around every tree, in every ditch and gully, with no results. "This is like looking for the proverbial needle in the haystack," Kira complained.

"Welcome to police work," Dallas shot back.

Dallas started writing notes on his hand.

"What are you doing?" she asked.

"Drawing a treasure map. If we can't figure out where it is, we need to make sure we know where it isn't. I don't want to search these fields more than once. Each road is a mile apart…."

Kira furrowed her brow. "How do you know that?"

"That's the way our forefathers set up the grid for most counties. Too bad cities had to break that tradition.

Which means Cody went at least two miles south of the house…." Dallas looked back toward the road and paused when he saw a maroon truck stop next to Kira's car. "You don't happen to recognize the pickup near your vehicle, do you?"

"No," she said promptly.

"It's probably the farmer, wondering what we're doing out here. Come here," he said, trying to sound casual.

She stepped toward Dallas. The truck drove past very slowly, turned onto the dirt road, then made a U-turn and drove back toward her car.

Kira's fingers dug into Dallas's forearm as he side-stepped to stay between her and the car. "You don't suppose it's the guy…Soprano, or whoever the big drug guy is, do you?"

"Sorento. No, the kingpin doesn't—" Just then they heard a loud bang.

Kira jumped a mile, digging her fingernails even deeper into his skin. "Was that him?"

Dallas tried not to sound alarmed, but even he was beginning to get suspicious. The car wouldn't do them much good with a flat tire. They had to move on, because he wasn't about to convince her not to change the tire now. Not with a drug dealer shooting at them.

"No," he lied. "Sounded like a car backfiring. Let's keep going toward the foster home." He pried her hand loose and held it tightly.

"Are you sure that wasn't a gun?" Kira said, tugging

her tennis shoe from the freshly turned farmland as he led her forward. "Hey, look. There are some bike tracks. That must be how Cody got clear out here and back so quickly."

Dallas pulled her close. "Looks more like a motorcycle of some kind," he said, picking up the pace. They came to the edge of the field and looked down a steep embankment into an irrigation canal. The pickup zoomed up the road toward them, "backfiring" as it approached.

"I don't think that was the truck engine," Kira said, her concern growing more evident. Dallas again put himself between her and the gun. He looked around for somewhere to take cover. The trees were on the other side of the canal, and there was only one way to cross it right now.

"Down into the canal, quick." He stepped off the edge and slid down the earthen side to the bottom. Kira was still standing at the top, well out of his reach. "Come on!"

"Thank goodness I hadn't changed into my church clothes yet." As Kira said it, she took that leap of faith.

"At least they haven't started running water yet!" Dallas said as he caught her at the bottom. They took off running, hoping the driver didn't figure out they were down in the canal channel. Dallas took hold of her hand again, practically dragging her along. He heard the rattle of the truck, which screeched to a stop on the gravel road sixteen feet above them.

Dallas wasn't sure if the shooter had a handgun or a rifle, but he only had one prayer. *Keep us safe, God.* Looking up, he saw a man sixty feet away, on the other side of a barbed-wire fence. A minute later, they heard shots fired again, and Dallas pushed Kira ahead of him. "Run faster, Kira. I don't think that's the landowner checking to be sure we're okay. There's a culvert ahead. Get in there and stay there," he demanded.

"I hate bugs and rodents."

"There isn't really a choice. A gun, or the protection of a dirty culvert." They reached the opening and Kira paused, then ducked into it.

"You aren't even winded!" she said as she gasped for air. She knelt down. "Don't you have your gun?"

He crouched next to her and tried to listen for the truck, or see if the shooter had followed them into the canal. "Of course I do, but I'm not going to get into a gunfight with you right next to me." He pulled his gun from the small of his back and started to move closer to the opening. "Stay in here, just in case."

"No, don't you dare go back out there. I didn't mean I wanted you to protect me. I…I just wondered." She jumped up and ran toward him. "Please, Dallas, don't go."

"I have to—" He felt the ground above them rumble as a vehicle drove over. "He headed west, so we're going back east again. There should be a small steel pipe running across the canal somewhere past where we dived in. It may have a wooden plank over it, but they're old and wobbly, so we need to be careful."

"I know, we used to play on them at my uncle's farm, but don't you dare tell my parents."

"Like they're going to punish you now?" Dallas said with a chuckle. "Run until you get to it, and climb back up and go to the nearest house."

She grabbed his hand. "What are you going to do?"

"I'll be behind you. If we hear the clatter of the truck, I'm going to fire. You just keep running. Don't stop for anything. Understand?"

She nodded, fear etched across her face. Kira ran, ignoring the uneven ground. Dallas sidestepped, watching the rim of the embankment for the shooter. *God, don't let me shoot an innocent bystander,* he prayed.

A vehicle approached, but went on by.

"Keep going," Dallas said as he caught up with her. "It's not the truck."

Ahead, Kira could see the pipe. "Are you sure we should try to go across that thing? I was considerably smaller when I went on them as a kid." She looked over her shoulder, comforted to know he was just a few steps behind.

"I'm hoping we won't have to go across it. We should be able to climb up the side to the road. Then we'll have to get over the barbed-wire fence, through the borrow ditch, then to the road." The one-foot-wide footbridge above the pipe was supported on each end by old pieces of broken concrete that had been piled there as cheap pylons.

"I've got to start exercising more often," Kira panted.

Dallas took hold of her hand as she started to climb up the embankment. "Wait," he said quietly as he examined the old concrete, tugging on several pieces to make sure it was secure. "I'll go first, then I can pull you up."

"What if he's waiting up there?" she whispered.

"That's the other reason I'm going first," he said as he holstered his gun again.

Dallas made it as far as the pipe, then had to maneuver around it before studying the situation again. He planted his foot on the dried mud on one side, gingerly rested his arm on the plank and lifted himself onto it. The wood groaned with his weight.

"That doesn't sound good," Kira called softly.

He peered over the edge of the canal embankment and looked both directions. "It's clear. Come on," he said as he lay prone on the planks. The wood continued to protest.

"I meant the footbridge doesn't sound like it's going to hold you."

"It only has to do so on a little while longer. Come on, before it decides to give up."

Kira thanked God again that she had not come dressed for church. She scrambled up to the pipe without a problem, but looked at Dallas with trepidation when she saw the condition of the rotting wood. "How about if you get on the side of the ditch instead."

"We're fine, just take my hand for support and climb onto the dirt."

She let go with one hand and lost her balance, tumbling to the bottom again. Dallas peered down at her. "You okay?"

She sat up and started up the side again. "Yeah, I'm fine." *I think.* This time, she made it far enough to grasp his hand before she started sliding again.

"Don't let go," he demanded. Dallas squeezed her hand and grabbed her other arm, twisting his body to keep hold of her. The wood protested with a small snap. Dallas propped himself on his elbows and crawled to solid ground, Kira dangling from his hands. He backed away from the canal embankment as it crumbled beneath them. She felt Dallas's strong hands squeezing hers tighter with each movement he made, pulling her with him. Finally, they were both back on solid ground.

Dallas collapsed into the dirt and took a deep breath. "Remind me to report that bridge to the water district." He pulled his phone from his pocket and dialed the police department. "Sarge, I need you to put out a BOLO for a maroon pickup, Ford F-250, in the area of County Road 86 and 19."

While Dallas explained the situation to the Sergeant, Kira rested her forearms on her knees, trying to catch her breath. The reality that someone had just fired at them began to sink in. She felt numb at the thought.

She looked around, wondering which was closer, the house or her car. Where was that maroon pickup now? Was the driver going to come back to finish them off, or had he just been trying to scare them away? And what did he want?

When Dallas finished his phone call, they headed toward the Woods house again. "I think we're closer to the car, Dallas," Kira told him. "Even if we have to go all the way around the field."

"We're not going back to the car. Even if it's there, it's most likely not operational anymore. That first shot was probably meant to disable it."

Kira stared at Dallas. She had never felt so overwhelmed. Thoughts she had never considered ran through her mind as she crossed the dirt road and entered the next field. They'd crossed one plowed field and one that still had corn stubble in it before they reached the outbuildings of the Woods farm.

Dallas hadn't said a word. Kira turned to be sure he was still behind her, even though she'd heard the crunch of cornstalks under his feet. His mouth twisted and he raised his eyebrows.

"Don't look at me like that," she declared.

Dallas shrugged. "Like what?"

"Like you want to say 'I told you so.' I was doing my job, not trying to do yours. Cody was missing and Deb phoned me. She didn't call the police."

Dallas took hold of her wrist and pulled her into his strong arms. "I wasn't going to say I told you so. I wasn't even thinking it. I was thinking that I hope we live to have a second date."

"A first date," she corrected, tears threatening to blind her. "I want a first date. Pizza and a movie on my living room floor is not a date!" Kira stomped past the barn, through the corrals and to the back door of the house, while Dallas repeated his apologies about going back to find the silver car.

"Kira," he said again.

She jiggled the doorknob to see if it happened to be unlocked. It didn't surprise her too much that it wasn't. She turned around to go back down the steps, but Dallas blocked her way and once more pulled her to him.

He looked her in the eye, then kissed her forehead. "I think if we make it to that first date, we may as well get married and skip the rest—" Dallas heard the familiar clank and clatter of the loose muffler on the truck. "Hide!" He pulled Kira behind the hedge of lilac bushes with him. The maroon truck rattled toward them, slowing down as it approached the house. It sped off again as soon as it was past.

Kira felt as if her heart was speeding along with it.

Dallas pulled out his cell phone and started pressing buttons as he pushed his way through the hedge.

"Who are you calling now?"

"I'm taking a picture. Let's hope someone at the Fossil Creek PD owes your brother a favor."

SEVENTEEN

Dallas and Kira sat on the front porch, waiting for her brother, Nick, to arrive to give them a ride into town. Kira called the Woodses and told them to find a place to stay in town for the night. Somewhere safe, she reiterated more than once.

"What were we talking about, before the truck came back?" Dallas asked. That was his first mistake.

"You had the nerve to ask me to marry you. Was that supposed to be a proposal?"

That was his second mistake. Answering would be his third. Dallas held up his hands in surrender. "I take it that's a no?"

Her jaw dropped and she stood up and walked away. She went ten yards, then back five. "What is wrong with this picture?" She huffed. "I don't even know where to start!"

Dallas knew it wasn't funny, but he wanted to laugh. He hadn't meant for her to take it seriously. Not really.

It probably wasn't a wise decision to admit that right now. "I make jokes when I'm stressed. Bad jokes, maybe," he said with a shrug. He went closer and touched her arm, but she jerked away. Was she that angry, or was she hurt?

Before they could finished their discussion, a sheriff's officer stopped by to make sure they were okay. He'd been sent out to look for the truck, and offered them a ride back to Kira's car. "Thanks anyway, Jarred. Her brother's already on the way. He should be here soon."

"I'll be close by. Call if you need anything," the deputy told them as he drove off.

Kira's brother Nick drove up in his unmarked car minutes after the sheriff left. He greeted them with a critical eye and a simple nod. Dallas could tell Kira was still fuming. The muscles in her jaw were strained and her usually plump lips were pulled into a thin line. Her normally light brown skin had a pale ashen look to it. She was covered in dirt, as Dallas was.

"What happened to you two?" Nick asked as he opened the back door.

Dallas waited, but Kira didn't say a word. "We had a lead on the cell phone, so we came looking for it," he explained. "Someone else apparently had the same tracking going on, because we had company."

Kira limped to the car and dropped into the back seat. Dallas knelt next to her, while her brother hovered nearby. "Kira, are you okay?" Dallas asked.

She nodded silently.

Nick tapped him on the head. When Dallas looked up, he saw concern and silent questions on her brother's face.

Dallas knew one way to determine if she was thinking clearly. "Would you like to go out to dinner and a movie tomorrow night? If I have to hire bodyguards to assure we can enjoy ourselves, I will." He rocked back on his heels, expecting her reaction.

"I think I'm busy. I'm going to a PTSD group at church. I think I'm going to need it."

She took his breath away. Even after all she'd been through, she remembered a scheduled meeting. "Let's get going, honey." He lifted her legs into the car and closed the door. "I'm going to sit back here with her," he told Nick. "Let's stop by the E.R. first, get her checked out."

"I think that's wise. What happened?"

As Dallas walked around the car, he filled Nick in on the highlights—the gunfire, the irrigation canal and Kira's tumble down the embankment. "Maybe she hit her head," Dallas said as he opened the door.

Kira seemed lethargic when he sat down next to her and tried talking to her. She smiled slightly and slumped against him.

"Make sure she stays conscious," Nick said. He spun the car out of the farmyard and turned on his siren.

Dallas struggled to get her seat belt fastened around her before he fastened his own. "She seemed okay twenty minutes ago. She did kind of lose her temper with me, but I just figured I had it coming. Maybe that was a reaction to the fall. Let's stop at the new hospital. I think that will be quicker to get to than going all the way into Fossil Creek."

Nick agreed. "So what is it you have on this shooter? Did you recognize him?"

Dallas brushed Kira's hair from her face so he could see her eyes. "We were never close enough to get a good look at him." He interrupted his discussion with Nick. "Kira? Kira, wake up." He roused her from her sleep. "Kira, who am I?"

She looked up at him and mumbled his name, then snuggled close again.

"That's comforting. She remembers who you are," Nick said.

"You're telling me!" Dallas hugged her close. "So anyway, we never made direct contact with the shooter, and I only have a lousy picture of the pickup. Hopefully you have better equipment than ours in Antelope Springs. This photo is going to take a lot of cleaning up to read the license plate."

"I'll see what my computer geek can do," Nick said as he pulled up the emergency entrance. They helped Kira into the hospital, and waited for a doctor to examine her.

While the medical staff ran tests, Dallas showed Nick the photo on his phone. "I didn't want to draw any more attention to Kira and myself, so the picture is pretty blurry. Do you think it can be cleared up enough to run the plates?"

"We'll see what the lab thinks. They have some new technology that might do it." Nick called the technician, who suggested they send it to him, and he'd see what he could do while they waited with Kira.

The doctor called Nick into the room, leaving Dallas out in the waiting area. It felt odd for Dallas to realize just how much he loved Kira. And yet because he wasn't a relative, he wouldn't be allowed to stay with her. He paced, blaming himself for her being hurt. A few minutes later, he took to the halls, where there was more room to pace, and burn off some of the adrenaline.

God, I beg you to take care of Kira. I was a fool to think I had any say in my future. I think she's right. I think you knew my heart was broken. I think you knew I was in no shape then to deal with returning to the uniform, let alone a relationship.

Dallas glanced out the window and saw the Rocky Mountains, topped with snow. He placed a fist on the steel frame of the window and leaned his forehead against the glass.

I didn't expect to find a woman who could empathize with what happened in my past, let alone someone who needs my help just as much as I need hers. Kira knows more than I do what it takes to maintain a relationship in law enforcement. Help her forgive me for how insen-

sitive I was to propose to her in the middle of this case. If you are really preparing us for one another, Father, hit me over the head when it's the right time to ask her to share my life. Give me the strength not to rush her, Lord.

He took a deep breath, wishing that this case was over so they could enjoy getting to know one another.

Dallas felt a tap on his shoulder. "Kira wants to see you."

Kira wanted to get back to her normal routine. No, actually, she wanted to move on. She'd been stuck in this rut for months.

She wanted to feel again, to fall in love. Problem was, the man she wanted seemed terrified of letting anyone into his life. He was so afraid of it he made jokes about getting married.

Nick patted her arm. "How're you doing, sis?"

Kira shrugged, still drowsy. "I feel like I'm caught in a tornado. It just keeps going round and round, and every time I land, something else goes wrong." *Like love.* "Who are these crazy people and when are they going to leave me alone? Would you hand me my water?"

Nick helped her get a drink, then sat on the flimsy hospital chair and propped his fingertips together. "Now that Mickey's gone, there's got to be something else they're after. I don't know. Maybe Mickey had his phone set up to move money from account to account, and the kingpin thinks he can move it electronically."

"This guy shot at us, more than once. Why is he trying to kill me?"

"I doubt he was trying to kill you," Nick said quietly. "Just scare you."

"Well, it worked," she said. "The guy in the truck wasn't just watching Dallas and me, he was checking out the Woodses house, too." Kira looked around. "Where is Dallas?"

"They wouldn't let him in the room with you. Only relatives. I know you've been through a lot together this last few weeks, but—"

"I want him here with me." She couldn't explain now.

"Kira," her brother admonished. "The hospital has rules."

"I know that, but he's going to be related," Kira said as the doctor walked in. "He asked me to marry him. I'm going to say yes. I need to tell him yes."

Nick's jaw dropped. "You're kidding."

"Would you go get him for me? And don't say anything yet, Nick. We want to break the news ourselves, in our own time. But that explains why I want him here. Please."

He stood up. "I'll be right back."

The doctor glanced at Kira. "When did this proposal take place?"

"A couple of hours ago, maybe." She noticed him writing something down. "You don't think I'm making things up, do you?"

"Well, I was thinking you may have a mild concussion, but if you're recalling details like that, a concussion is unlikely. That's the good news."

"And the bad?" She asked hesitantly.

"A broken scapula, which is pretty rare. You must have hit something directly."

"A chunk of cement, in an irrigation canal," she said, recalling the tumble she'd taken. "It hurt, especially when I climbed out of the ditch."

"You used your arm to climb, after the fall? No wonder you're in such pain." He wrote more notes, then looked at her again. "Your brother mentioned you were out of it when they brought you here. I previously thought that must have been a concussion, but it sounds like that was your defense mechanism kicking in. When you didn't listen to your brain telling you not to use your arm, it kicked into high gear, making you sleep."

"I thought you were going to wait to go through all of this until we got here," Nick said, interrupting the doctor. "What did you find?"

Dallas made a beeline for Kira's bedside. He leaned down and kissed her cheek. "You're not feeling any better, are you."

She shrugged one shoulder. "Not so good."

The doctor nodded. "We're just discussing how this may have happened. I was asking her questions as a point of reference."

Dallas looked into her drowsy eyes and brushed dirt from her jaw. "What's wrong with her?"

"She's on some pain medicine that will keep her resting for a while so we can monitor the bruise on her back and shoulder. She cracked her scapula in a fall, apparently." The doctor looked at Kira. "I'll need to ask—" he turned to Dallas "—you a few questions to verify she doesn't have any memory loss or confusion."

"I'm Dallas Brooks," he said, extending his hand, "and I'm happy to answer any questions if it will help."

Nick watched critically as Kira waited.

"How long ago would you say Kira fell?"

Dallas looked at his watch. "Two or three hours ago, I'd guess. We were climbing on some chunks of concrete. I asked if she was okay, and she said she thought so."

"A broken scapula is very rare. She thinks she hit a sharp corner of the concrete?"

"She might have. I couldn't see her very well. I was lying across a rickety old foot bridge to help pull her up an embankment. I heard her fall, and it didn't sound good, but then she popped right back up and climbed out."

The doctor wrote down a few more things, then looked up again. "You mentioned that she got upset with you at one point, which didn't seem normal to you."

Dallas nodded. "The yelling didn't seem like her, but it wasn't totally out of line. I was a little insensitive, and mentioned getting married."

"You think?" Nick mumbled.

"Yeah, I know. I figured she had a right to be upset, since came a little out of the blue. You think her outburst was due to something else?"

He shrugged. "Actually, I thought maybe she had a concussion, but she insisted we let you in, claiming that you're engaged."

EIGHTEEN

Dallas felt his heart beat faster. "Engaged, huh?" He smiled.

"So you really did propose? In the middle of all this? Are you crazy?" Nick asked in disbelief.

He chuckled. "Yeah, but she never said yes. That's when she started yelling. And I figured she had every right to yell. We'd just been shot at." He looked admiringly at her sleeping form. "And, well, we haven't gone through the traditional dating routine."

The doctor smiled. "Sounds like love at first sight. Congratulations. I hope it works out for you both." He filled Dallas and Nick in on Kira's condition, and how he wanted to make sure she stayed calm for a few days before dismissing her. "The break doesn't look that serious right now, but that bruise is pretty deep. If she's still in danger, a quiet hospital might be a good place for her to disappear for a few days."

Dallas couldn't believe she'd accepted his proposal. His heart swelled with love.

"She'll also be in pain, especially until we can immobilize that arm. I don't want to do that until the swelling has gone down. For now we've used a light wrapping of bandages to remind her not to move it, and to hold the ice in place. In about forty-eight hours we'll change that to heat to get the blood flowing through that bruised area again. We want to watch for clotting. In the meantime we'll give her medicine through her IV—"

"Doctor, sorry to interrupt, but I think you're going to have to go through all of this again for our parents, anyway. I'm going to call Mom and Dad, see if they can stay with her for the afternoon." Nick pulled out his cell phone.

"I'll stay with Kira," Dallas insisted.

"No way," Nick said. "You and I are going to find that kid and have a talk with him. If he won't give us the phone, he's going in the juvenile detention center. I've had it with his games."

"I'm not leaving her alone yet." Dallas had the impression that Nick wasn't in favor of their engagement. He couldn't blame him for his concerns. Dallas had plenty of his own, which would have to be dealt with another time. "Any word on the truck yet?"

"Yeah, they cleaned up the picture. The truck was stolen two weeks ago from a ranch south of Vail. No help at all."

Kira groaned, drawing her brother's attention and Dallas's. "Don't let them take Cody and Betsy from Deb and Glen. It wouldn't be good for the Woodses. And besides, I can't separate the kids. I promised they would stay together."

"What do you mean, it wouldn't be good for Deb and Glen?" her brother asked. "They know this is part of the deal. I mean, kids from good homes aren't typically sent to foster care, but they can't be thrilled to have this danger invading their house." He held up his hand, motioning toward the phone. "Mom, Kira's been hurt and needs to stay in the hospital. Could you and Dad come stay with her until we can get police protection arranged?"

Their mother apparently hit the ceiling as Nick handed the phone to Kira.

"I'm going to be okay, Mom. Yeah," she said after a pause. "I know. Love you, too. I'll see you in a while and I'll explain it all then." Kira handed the phone to her brother. "You scared her to death, Nick. And cancel the police protection bit."

Both Dallas and Nick refused vehemently. Though Dallas felt guilty for arguing with her, he was not about to back down.

She didn't say a word. Kira didn't look like she had the energy left to argue.

"Who do we need to talk to in Protective Services to move the kids, Kira?" Nick pressed.

Dallas wondered if her supervisor was still the only person other than Kira who would be aware of Cody and Betsy's true location. He made a note to talk to her about that after Nick left. She needed to let them know she'd be out of the office, and that it was an injury due to the requirements of the job. When his mind came back to Nick and Kira, they were back to the argument about the Woodses keeping the kids.

"Deb and Glen are the best foster parents we have in the county. They were ready to adopt three siblings they had taken into their foster care. The mother got out of prison a week before the adoption went through, and they've spent the last year teaching the mother how to parent. Instead of fostering the children, they fostered the family."

Nick wouldn't let it go. "That's admirable, but this is different, Kira."

"Not really. So many times we see well-meaning foster families try to sabotage parents' efforts to get their kids back. Not this couple. They worked for months with the mother, showing her how to be a mom and create a good home for her children."

Kira shifted in the bed, wincing when she tried to move the right side of her body. "They took the mother to church with them, and gave their hearts to the family. It took months for them to be ready to open their home again. In spite of our problems with Cody, this is the absolute best place for him. They've been working hard with both kids. They won't stop now."

Dallas recognized the look on her brother's face—a mixture of fear and pride. Mostly fear. "I admire your determination to keep Cody and Betsy together, Kira, but it's gone beyond what's safe, for anyone. You're in the hospital with injuries that could have been a lot worse. We need to seriously consider moving Cody to a detention center where he can't just come and go and disappear like this. Even if it's only temporary."

She tried to adjust the pillow behind her, and glared at Dallas. "I should have known you'd argue with me."

"We're not arguing with you. We're being realistic, Kira. I feel for the Woodses. I even feel for Cody," Nick said.

Kira glanced at Nick, then back to Dallas. "Cody and Betsy couldn't ask for a better home," she said defensively.

"We're not disputing that, Kira," Dallas said gently as he helped her sit up. He rearranged the pillow behind her. "It's also putting the foster family at risk. We can't trust Cody. He turned his own mother in. He's not being honest with anyone. How can we trust him not to turn on the Woodses?"

"He doesn't know how to trust anyone. He couldn't trust his own mother, Dallas." She stared into his blue eyes, as if hoping to make him understand. "That doesn't make him any less important in the eyes of God. He's scared of losing everyone he cares about."

Dallas turned away, rolling his head from side to side.

"Let me talk to him again, Dallas, please."

"You're staying right where you are. You refused to

step back, and now you're hurt. Surely you don't expect me to ignore that, do you?" he asked.

Kira crossed her free arm over the one that was tied to her body, and let out a gasp at the pain. She took a deep breath and glanced at her brother. "Nick?"

"Don't look at me," he exclaimed, holding his hands up. "From what I've heard in the last few weeks, you've probably given the kid more rope than he deserves. This case isn't one I wanted you involved with in the first place, Kira. I agree with Dallas."

She let her head fall back against the pillow, and took a deep breath. She was wearing herself out. "I still have a job to do, and so do you. I guess we're not going to be able to agree on this one," she argued, focusing on her brother, then turning to Dallas.

"I'm not backing away from my job," Dallas insisted. He took hold of her hand. "I'm not letting Cody know where you are, Kira. And you'd better not, either. He could make this a lot simpler if he'd open up. He's putting everyone around him at risk. Most of all you, because you're thinking with your heart and not your head." He looked at her brother. "Could I have a few minutes to talk to your sister alone, Nick?"

"Sure, talk some sense into her, would you?"

When Nick had left, Dallas paced the room like a caged animal, trying to decide what to say. "Kira…" He had no doubts about his feelings for her, but he didn't want her to think he was putting his emotions before his job. He didn't need to scare her to death. "I'm worried about you."

"I didn't ask you to…" She turned away.

"Unless you're changing your mind about my proposal, worrying about you goes with the commitment." He hesitated, surprised by her reaction. "I'm afraid of losing the chance to get to know you better, Kira. I realized you weren't interested in having another cop in your life, and I ignored that. I was selfish and only thinking of how much I adore you. I won't hold you to my proposal—"

"Whoa, wait just a minute," Kira said weakly. She gazed up at him. "That's not true." She smiled tentatively. "I never said anything about not wanting to date a cop. My brothers were trying to scare you away."

She continued to confuse him. "Yeah, that's clear, too. I don't want to see you hurt again," Dallas admitted.

"Hurt? By who? Cody?" Kira shook her head. "Dallas, this case has hit a soft spot for me. It reminds me of when my little brother, Jimmie, was taken away from me. I had no way to protect him. I've spent the last six months trying to find him, and for twenty years before that I've lived with the guilt of letting him down." Tears streamed from her eyes, and Dallas searched for a box of tissues.

Finally, Kira just wiped her face with the corner of her bedsheet. "I don't want Cody to go through that. I don't want Betsy to grow up feeling as if everyone abandoned her. Their dad ran off before Betsy was born, her mom is incapable of being a real mother to her, and her brother is the only one she has left. If I put Cody in a detention center…" She shook her head. "That will just reinforce the negative. He's trying to protect his sister, and I'm not going to let him down."

Dallas took a deep breath and let it out, praying that she would take what he had to say the right way. "I know that, Kira, but he's a kid. And he doesn't care about hurting you or anyone else. No, he obviously cares about Betsy. But if he would only realize that he's making matters worse by not trusting us, we could get to the bottom of this." He leaned against the rail of her bed and looked into her tired eyes.

Kira gazed back, and he could feel her love as she said, "God tells us to administer justice and take care of the poor and needy. It's clear that Cody is trying to get away from the trouble that his mother has been involved in. Being a teenager isn't a crime. He needs to have good examples to follow, not be punished for trying to take care of those less capable."

She was right. "As much as you want to help him, Kira, he doesn't seem willing to accept help."

"He's afraid. He doesn't know who he can trust," she stated.

"No, he probably doesn't. We've tried, and as difficult as it may be to accept it, sometimes we have to know when it's time to let go. We can't help him if he won't open up to us. I want the chance to worry about you, Kira. I need your promise that you won't take any more risks to try to help Cody."

"I can't give it to you." She closed her eyes and tears welled in the corners. "I assured him that I would keep him and Betsy together. I can't break my word to him, and I can't make a promise to you that I can't keep. I promised him first, Dallas."

Dallas sat on the hospital bed next to her. He brushed the dusty curls out of her eyes and wrapped his arms around her. "Oh, Kira," he said, realizing that it was too late. He should have gotten her out of his heart long before now. *This is why I didn't want to fall in love again. Someone always gets hurt.*

He couldn't expect her to stop trying to heal others, any more than he could walk away from law enforcement.

Kira looked up into his eyes as he cautiously lowered his lips to hers. She tried to calm her racing heart, but it was pointless. The sweetness of his kiss mesmerized her. It was impossible that she'd fallen so hopelessly in love. They'd known each other such a short time. It had only been a few weeks ago that she'd gone on that ride-along.

She tightened her hug and realized suddenly that he was wearing his Kevlar vest. Kira pushed herself out of his embrace. "You're off duty. Why…" Her hand skimmed over his chest. "Why are you wearing your vest?"

He seemed puzzled. "What's wrong with me wearing my bulletproof vest?"

"Do you always wear it off duty?"

Dallas's hands fell away from her shoulders and he stepped back, crossing his arms over his chest. "No," he said with annoyance. "But you cancelled going to church." He ran his hand over his chin, his agony clear in his eyes. "I put it on because we were going to look for Cody. I wear it any time I suspect there could be trouble. And with anything connected to Cody, I expect trouble. I'm sorry if that sounds paranoid, but considering what happened the other night I didn't want to let them slip through her fingers again. We don't know who we're dealing with, I'd rather be prepared than dead."

Kira felt a shiver tickle her spine. "I guess you don't plan to be shot at any day, even when you go to work…."

"If it makes a difference, I didn't expect to propose to you today, either, but I'm a man of my word. You can still say no, but I don't regret letting you know my intentions."

His eyes challenged hers, and then settled on her lips as he pulled her close again.

Kira pushed him away, laughing this time. "Not when you're wearing a bulletproof vest!"

"So?"

"Next time you kiss me, there'd better not be any hint of guns or reminders of bulletproof vests."

"You must be willing to wait awhile, then, huh?"

"Not especially," she said seriously, "But I don't want

this image of you shielding your heart from me when I'm totally vulnerable to letting you in." She tapped her own heart. "I expect open access." She watched as Dallas backed away. "And just to make myself perfectly clear, Dallas, the only cop I'm interested in dating or marrying is you."

Their conversation was interrupted by a sharp knock, followed by Nick clearing his throat as he walked through the door. "The deputy sheriff found the pickup a few miles away from the Woods house. From the skid marks, looks like he was going too fast when he hit the gravel road. There's some blood, but no sign of the driver yet."

NINETEEN

"Why don't you go ahead and take a look, Nick. I'm not leaving until someone else arrives to stay with Kira. We're not that far from the Woodses' farm. If the guy is on foot, he may come to the hospital for treatment. I'll send a warning to the E.R. nurses about him, and to keep quiet about Kira's presence here." Dallas held her hand as the IV machine buzzed, dispensing Kira's next dose of pain medication.

"I've called to ask for police protection here."

"Nick…" Kira started to argue, then shook her head instead. "Never mind. It's two against one."

Dallas squeezed her hand gently and turned back to her brother. "I can call you before I make arrangements to talk to Cody, if you'd like to go with me. Besides, I think it's time I talk to your dad."

"Good luck with that, and by the way, both of you, congratulations. I'm really happy for you two." Nick shook Dallas's hand. "I'd say don't rush into anything, but then again, you could end up like me, a chronic bachelor. When you find the right one, you can't take love for granted." He bent down and gave Kira a kiss. "You better behave in here, sis, or you're not going to have any energy to plan a wedding."

Kira reached out and took Dallas's hand. "I don't ever plan to take this man for granted. Thanks, Nick. I told Dallas you're all just trying to scare away the wrong guy. I think he passed your test with flying colors."

"And here we thought we were so sly."

After her brother left, Kira dozed off, leaving Dallas waiting for her mom and dad to arrive. When they did, he realized this was his last chance to back out. "Afternoon, Mr. and Mrs. Matthews."

"Hello, Officer Brooks," Ted said gruffly as he shook Dallas's clammy hand. "Care to explain what happened to my little girl?"

Dallas understood now why Nick had been all too happy to leave him here with Kira. "Sure, but first, please call me Dallas. Did Nick explain what the doctor said?"

"Nah, he was off after someone fleeing the scene. I'm a little confused why you're here with Kira, and not out looking for this yahoo who shot at you."

Dallas wondered if Nick had told them about the engagement. "I'll explain that, too. Mainly…" The words wouldn't come.

"She's a mess! What happened?" Grace asked as she tucked unruly curls away from her daughter's face.

Dallas offered Kira's mother the chair, but she refused. "I want to be right here when she wakes up. You go ahead and tell us what happened, Dallas." She stood next to the hospital bed, where Dallas had spent the last two hours.

"Well," he said, taking a deep breath, "Kira's doctor thinks she cracked her scapula. She has a deep bruise from a fall, and they're hoping the break will heal without having to brace it. As you can see, they've immobilized her arm to keep her from moving it. They have ice packs under the wrap to help the swelling go down. She's in quite a bit of pain, so they are giving her regularly timed doses of medicine so she can rest and stay still."

"Good, she never would stay still when she was sick. They figured her out quickly, didn't they?" her mother said.

"I suppose she was after that kid again, wasn't she?" her father admonished. "I knew this case was going to hit home for her. She has such a stubborn streak."

Dallas nodded. "She got a call from the foster mother, so we went out to look for Cody." He finished the story about the chase and how she'd fallen onto the broken concrete.

"I hope you had the sense to wear your vest out here," her father commented.

"Much to Kira's displeasure, yes, I did." After she'd yelled at him, he'd taken it off, and it now rested on the floor, behind the recliner.

Her dad glanced at it, then back at Dallas. "So she's going to have to stay here a few days?"

Dallas nodded. "Yes, sir."

"You going to be here with her the whole time?" Her dad must have been a great cop, too.

"I plan on being here as much as possible, sir. I couldn't live with myself if something else happened to her. Which brings me to why I'm here instead of Nick." He took a deep breath. "Kira is a very special woman."

As if she heard them talking, Kira moaned.

They all turned toward the bed, waiting. But she didn't wake up. "Falling in love was about the last thing I intended, especially in the middle of a case we're both tied up in," Dallas said, staring at Kira. "While we've been working the case, we've discovered we have a lot in common. But today, as we were trying to keep each other safe, I realized I want to spend every day with Kira." He turned his attention to Grace, then Ted. "I'd like to ask your permission to court your daughter, with the full intention of marrying her."

They were both silent.

"Does she know about this?" her father asked bluntly.

Dallas laughed. "Yes, she does. I probably should have chosen a better time to tell her how I feel, because she started yelling at me."

Her parents laughed, too. Grace had tears streaming down her face. "That's my daughter," she said.

"The hospital wasn't going to let me in to see her. She told them we're engaged, so they'd let me be here."

Ted shook his hand. "I'm guessing that's why the vest is now sitting on the floor?"

"Yes, sir. I'm learning the rules," he said with a smile. "I expect when she's off these medications, she may come up with a few more. That's okay, I'm a quick study."

"As long as you're learning the rules, I think you'd better drop the 'sir' and learn to call me Dad."

"I'll work on that…Dad." It felt odd, saying it. His own father had died right before Dallas went into the academy, shot in the line of duty.

Grace ran around the bed and threw her arms around Dallas. "I knew she had her heart twisted into a knot over someone. Welcome to the family, Dallas."

Kira woke, the pain in her right shoulder intense. "Hi," she said to Dallas, who was beaming down at her. "What are you still doing here? I thought you'd be out catching the bad guys."

"I wanted one kiss before I left." He leaned over the rail of her bed, and she put her hand up to stop him. As if he read her mind, he said, "No vest guarding my heart—so can I kiss my fiancée?"

She smiled. "You're learning how to woo me." Kira's one good arm circled around him and pulled him closer.

Dallas's kiss was the best pain reliever she could

have asked for, and she didn't want it to end. "That was definitely worth the wait. I can't wait for more," she whispered.

He trailed little kisses along her jaw, to her ear. "You'll have to. Your parents are here to stay with you while I'm gone."

Kira let go of his shirt, but he pressed her against the bed.

"Don't move so quickly," he said softly. "Remember your shoulder blade is broken." Then he backed away and put his hand on the button to raise the head of the bed. "Why don't you call the nurse, see if the doctor is here to explain things to you and your parents?"

"Uh…" she said to her folks, remembering the night she and Kent had made the joke about a shotgun wedding. "Sorry about that, I didn't know you were here."

Her mother smiled. "We figured that out. But I guess it's to be expected for an engaged woman to feel that way about her fiancé, isn't it?"

Kira beamed, feeling the blush deepen. "Yeah, but I really don't want to discuss it with you and Dad here…."

"Thank you," Ted said with a smile.

Dallas walked over to pick up his vest. "And I'd better get hold of the Woodses to talk to Cody. Where'd they put your cell phone when they checked you in?"

"They put everything in a bag. Is it in the closet?"

Her mother opened the door and looked. "It's not here. Maybe Nick took it."

A quick call to Nick settled that. He hadn't taken anything; the nurses had moved her upstairs.

"I just called the Woodses' house and left a message for them there," she added. "I don't have a cell phone number for them."

"How were you going to reach them?" he asked.

"They were going to call my cell phone when they decided where to go."

Dallas let out a deep breath. "Let's hope we can hear your phone ringing. If nothing else, maybe one of the nurses will answer." He waited a few minutes, then shook his head. "Nothing."

"Dad, would you mind checking with the desk, see if they can track down my belongings?" Kira asked.

Dallas dialed another number. "Hi, this is Dallas Brooks. Would you send a car to the main entrance of the new hospital?" He turned to Kira. "I'm going to go out to the Woodses' place and make sure things are okay there. Call if you hear from them. Otherwise, I'll assume they're in hiding, and I'll talk to Cody in the morning at school." He pulled his polo shirt off, and Kira was surprised to find he had a dark T-shirt underneath.

"What are you doing?"

"Putting my vest back on. It's bad enough to wear it around off duty, but nothing sends panic through a hospital emergency room like a man carrying a Kevlar vest."

"Oh," she said. "Well then, give me one more kiss before you put it back on."

Dallas moved across the floor quickly. Was he as eager as she to finally share their feelings openly? He kissed her warmly.

He jotted his cell number on her tissue box, next to the phone. "Call anytime," he said with a smile. He deftly put his vest on and fastened it over the T-shirt.

"Huh," she said, watching with amazement. "I never realized cops wear two shirts. Did you know that, Mom?"

"Judging by the laundry your dad came home with, yes, I figured it out. Most men change at the station, so I never actually saw your father put his vest on. Interesting little details I never knew I was missing, even with four police officers in the family. Oops—make that five."

Dallas smiled. "I feel like I'm disclosing top secret information or something."

"Now you know why I want open access." Kira grinned mischievously. "Be careful, Dallas."

"And you, behave," he said as he pulled his polo shirt over the vest. "I love you."

TWENTY

Dallas hurried down the stairs to the front desk just as the Antelope Springs police car showed up. "What's going on?" Sergeant Shaline asked.

Dallas explained all that had happened. "I'm going to be on surveillance outside the Woodses' place tonight. I'd like to check out a set of night-vision goggles."

"That's out of our jurisdiction. Call the sheriff's office and see if they have someone who can assist."

"How about an officer from the county drug task force? He's on the Fossil Creek force. He knows more about the drug side of this, and already has contacts working on the Zelanski case."

Shaline laughed. "I see you've met Kira's family, huh?"

"Yeah. In fact…" Dallas paused, hesitant to spread the news too quickly. His doubts had vanished, but he didn't know if hers would reappear after she came off her medication. "I've met them all, thanks to your advice to put out a BOLO on her."

"You did it?" he asked incredulously.

"No. I didn't, but someone had broken into her condo, and I called in the Fossil Creek department. The responding officer was a greenhorn who didn't realize she had brothers on the force, either. *He* did it."

The two had a good laugh as they drove to the station. As Dallas was checking out a car and equipment, Shaline contacted the county sheriff to let him know what was going on.

The sergeant returned with some paperwork. "It's all set up. Your future brother-in-law says he's bringing sandwiches."

Dallas froze. Shaline was testing him, that was clear. When Dallas remained speechless, his colleague laughed. "All I have to say is 'You're welcome!' Kent and I have been working on this for months. But the incident with Mickey was not part of the plan. Just the matchmaking part."

Dallas laughed in turn. "You didn't."

"Afraid so," he said, dancing around his office with his arms in the air, as if signaling a touchdown.

Dallas shook his head and turned to go.

"Congratulations. And be careful out there tonight. You've got a great lady waiting for you."

"Yes, I do," he said without glancing back. "You may have won a bet, Shaline, but I get the prize." He let the door slam behind him.

He called Kira on his way to the Woods house.

They'd found her phone, but hadn't heard anything from the family yet.

Next he called Kent, to confirm their location to meet. "Kira hasn't heard anything from the Woods family," Dallas told him. "Any word from Nick on the driver of the pickup?"

"Yeah, he's out of the picture. I'll fill you in on that later." There was an odd tone to Kent's voice.

"What's wrong?" Dallas asked. "We're going out into the country, and pretty soon it's going to be dark. I don't want another replay of this morning. I've had enough thrown at me today."

"What else happened?" Kent asked.

"I found out about you and Shaline setting me up. From the way Nick and Garrett reacted, I doubt they knew you were behind it all."

"Surely you're not going to complain about that? I hear you popped the question today."

"And she accepted. So back to business. I'm about at the Woodses' house. What's up with the guy? I don't want any more surprises."

Kent groaned. "What do you know about Kira's brother Jimmie?"

"Just that she has one, and she's been trying to find him. Why?"

"He's a scumbag, and I've known where he was all along. He broke out of a California prison a couple of days ago, somehow got to Colorado. Probably been involved with Raul Sorento. I'm guessing he hooked up with one of Raul's men in prison. When Nick heard who reported that maroon pickup stolen, he called, and found out Jimmie Driscoe had worked for this rancher a year or so ago."

Dallas pulled off the road to finish listening to the story.

"The guy said he caught him hot-wiring it. Jimmie gave him some hard luck story about why he'd left. He said he was looking for his sister and needed to get to Fossil Creek. The rancher refused to hire him back on, and Jimmie coldcocked him and took off. Apparently there was a truck broken down on the interstate that was registered to one of Raul's mules.

"The rest is a little unclear. I think they got here, and Jimmie found out about the missing drugs, and the search for the kid with the phone. Either he was told to go get it from this farm, or he overheard someone and thought he could make some easy money."

"So who was chasing us?" Dallas asked. "Jimmie? Why would he shoot at Kira?"

"He probably doesn't know what his sister looks like now. You can ask him tomorrow. He's in jail, sobering up. Nick and the sheriff caught him as he tried to climb out of the irrigation canal. As usual, he was drunker than a skunk. He claims Cody knows where the money and the dope are, and that someone is meeting the boy tonight."

Just then, Dallas saw Kent's car pass by.

"Follow me," Kira's brother said. "I'll drive like a drunk, and you pull me over."

Dallas screeched ahead, turning on his lights right after Kent began swerving. He hoped he didn't do too good of a job acting. It would be easy to lose control on the dirt road. "Stop, you idiot."

"I will. I'm waiting till we get to the Woodses' farm. Then I'll escape, and you can disappear, looking for me. Be sure to take your keys and lock up the car. Oh, and you might want to grab your ammo."

"What?"

"If you're after a felon, you have to make it look real, don't you?"

"You are crazy."

"I'm a narc. Of course I'm a bit crazy."

Dallas didn't like this at all. Everything went as planned, and he caught up with his 'felon' in the Woodses' barn. He'd managed to tuck his night-vision goggles into his shirt before he stopped Kent, then pulled his shotgun and ammo from the trunk before he took off chasing him.

Dallas wondered if anyone watching would think a cop running off after a drunk driver was fishy, but he hoped they bought it. He climbed the ladder to the hayloft and threw his gear ahead of him, then collapsed next to Kent.

"Are the Woodses at home?" he panted, out of breath.

"Yes," Kent said, "but it's my team. After Kira called

Nick from the farm, he called me. I followed the Woodses home from church and got it all set up. Congratulations, by the way. I knew you two would hit it off."

The guy was definitely crazy, being able to mix family life and the insane existence of an undercover narcotics officer.

"So where's Cody?" Dallas put on his goggles and looked around.

"He's downtown with the family. We'll tail him."

"And if we already have Cody, don't we have the phone?"

"Cody claims he set up the exchange out here so no one would be around. He's giving them the phone, but it has one of our tracker chips in it. We have the original chip, and have already found the money. The DEA is following the trail and is setting up the sting as we speak. Cody told Sorento that he'd meet them at the tractor in the field out there. I had Cody paint a peace sign on it so we can find it in the dark."

"Sorento, the kingpin? You really think he's going to meet Cody?"

"No, but I'm prepared, just in case," Kent said.

Four hours later, they were still sitting in the pitch-black barn, waiting. Cody hadn't showed up, and the trail never saw him leave the hotel.

"I'm heading over to the school," Dallas said finally. It had been thirty minutes since the exchange was to have taken place. "Are you sure Cody hasn't had any phone calls since you set this plan in motion? Maybe Sorento caught wind of the sting and changed the location."

"We've put money in a suitcase under the tractor. He'll show."

"You wait here, then. I'm going to follow my hunch."

Kent protested as Dallas quietly went down the ladder, wearing his goggles and the helmet that Kent had waiting for a backup officer. "Tell your team that it's me going around the house to my car."

"You get yourself killed, and my sister will never forgive me."

Dallas hunched over to stay behind the hedge of lilacs, and ran to the police cruiser. He hadn't seen a sign of anyone yet. He looked into the back of the vehicle before unlocking the door, then underneath to make sure no one was waiting to ambush him. The coast was clear.

He tore out, lights and siren blazing, headed for the high school. As Kent discussed Cody, Dallas had realized the one place he regularly saw the teen hang out was near the west side of the campus, where large pine trees and a statue of the school mascot stood. It had taken several days before Dallas had figured out there was one blind spot where he couldn't see Cody. And the boy had used that to his benefit. It would make a perfect location to meet a drug dealer. Cody didn't just want the kingpin caught, he wanted rid of him altogether, so no one would bother him or Betsy again.

Dallas turned off his lights and siren a few blocks

away and stopped before he reached the school parking lot. Dallas jogged toward the school, staying in the shadows. *Where's the spotlight that's usually on the mascot?* Dallas wondered. When he put on the goggles, he noticed someone standing near the statue. Was it Cody? Or Sorento?

Dallas took a deep breath and let it out softly, in and out again, trying to slow his racing heart. *God, guide me through the darkness and lead me to Sorento.*

Scanning the area through the goggles, he spotted someone walking down the block toward the statue. He sighted in his shotgun and found them, then removed the goggles.

He was too far away. He looked around, wondering what else he could use as cover. He recalled the location of a tree and a trash can. *Not quite a shield of armor, God, but you've had less to work with.* He eased forward.

Each step sounded louder than the previous one. He stopped, but the noise continued. It wasn't him making it.

He saw Cody running toward the statue. Shots fired and the youth fell. Dallas put the shotgun to his shoulder and trained it on a bulky figure. "So, kid, where's the real phone? This isn't Mickey's."

"That's the one I took from him." Cody ducked behind the statue, between Dallas and Sorento. "Maybe his was with the money. I told you we had to meet at the tractor."

"You know as well as I do that we'd have had all sorts

of company there. I wasn't born yesterday." The kingpin took a step around the statue and Dallas took aim.

"Sorento," Dallas yelled, "you're surrounded. Drop your weapons!" Cody jumped up and ran, and Dallas fired. The man collapsed, crumpling to the ground.

"Brooks?"

"Cody, stay put! You're in deep trouble."

"Better that than dead," the kid said.

Dallas eased closer to the body, tossing a rock next to his hand to make sure he wasn't playing dead. Sorento didn't move. It shouldn't have been this easy. Surely the man had been wearing a vest. Dallas kicked Sorento's foot, his Glock ready to fire if the man flinched. "Sorento, I'm not naive enough to believe that one shot killed you, but make me fire again, and I'm not going to settle for anything less."

Just then, Sorento rolled over and reached for the gun in his waistband.

Dallas shot, and as promised, he didn't waste anyone's time.

He called the station, but no sooner had he dialed than two cars arrived. "Cody? Did you call them?"

"Sure as shooting I did. If he'd have shot you, Sorento would have killed me in an instant, and then who'd have taken care of Betsy?"

"What you did was irresponsible, Cody. We were trying to help you."

"I was more afraid of Sorento than I was of you or

even Social Services. You seen what they put my mom through?"

As soon as his fellow officers were there to cover the body, Dallas stepped over the dead kingpin and gathered Cody in his arms.

"What phone did you use? I thought you gave the one to Sorento."

"He just said it wasn't the right one. I never said he had a working phone."

TWENTY-ONE

After they'd finished filling out paperwork, Dallas made a trip to visit Jimmie Driscoe to find out his involvement with Sorento. He found Garrett already there, waiting for them to bring Jimmie to the visitors' area.

"Hi, I just left Nick and Kent at the sheriff's office," Dallas said.

Yeah, they told me you'd probably come over here." Garrett smiled. "I hear congratulations are in order. I knew there was something going on that night at her condo."

"Thanks, but there wasn't anything going on. At that point, we'd just met the one time when she rode along."

Her brother looked skeptical. "You're serious? So have you gone out every night since, or what?"

"Just a couple attempts, but even those were interrupted by the investigation."

"And you asked Kira to marry you? You hardly know her. She has a temper."

Dallas laughed. He didn't even have to question

himself again. "I know that. A temper isn't such a bad thing if it's used appropriately. It got her through a lot these last few weeks. She has a lot of other strengths, too, Garrett. It's amazing what you learn about a person going through something like this. I've never been so sure of a decision in my life."

"I've never believed in that 'love at first sight' theory myself, but I could see she cared about you even that night as she chewed you out. Ooh-eee, she was mad." He laughed, then the smile disappeared from his face as the interrogation-room door rattled. "It's hard to believe she's related to this guy."

"Yeah," Dallas said as he watched the wiry, thin man stumble into the chair across from him and Garrett. "You Jimmie Driscoe?"

The man looked like he'd been awakened from a deep sleep. He nodded. "Yeah, who're you?"

"Dallas Brooks. I was with your sister when you shot at us this afternoon."

The man backed away, fear in his eyes. "You're the second person to tell me that woman out there was my sister. I can't believe it. I wasn't shooting at ya, for the record."

"I'm Garrett Matthews, Kira's brother. My family adopted Kira Driscoe as a little girl, and she had a brother James, whose uncle took him, but wouldn't take Kira. That sound familiar?"

"You ain't her brother," the man argued. "He's a cop."

Garrett pulled out his badge. "I'm another brother. I'm a cop, too. You must have met Nick. He's a detective."

"Nah, this guy wasn't Nick. He was older, kinda scruffy. Kelly, or Kirk?"

Dallas wanted to laugh. Wait till the poor guy found out all of them were cops.

Garrett did laugh. "Yeah, you're close. That was Kent. He's a cop, too. So is Kira's dad, and now, Kira's fiancé here, Dallas."

Jimmie shook his head and mumbled a swear word. "Ain't that just my lousy luck!"

"So, why were you shooting at us?" Dallas asked.

"I wasn't shooting at neither of ya. I was told to kill anyone going after some phone that was supposed to be hidden out there. Even though I didn't know who ya was, I wasn't about to kill anyone and get life in the pen, so I shot out the tires, tried to scare you a bit." He hid his face in his hands. "Probably why Chains McClennahan offered to bust me outta the pen in the first place. I'm sorry, man. I wasn't going to kill anyone, just scare them away so I could go find that BlackBerry gizmo, and pay off my debt to Sorento so his thugs will leave me alone."

Dallas filled him in on Sorento's fate, finding the stash of money, and asked whether any of Sorento's thugs would now take his place.

"No way," he insisted. "The only other person with his clout is already in the supermax for knocking off most of his mules and dealers when they turned on him. Is Kira okay?"

"She'll recover. You know she's been looking for you?" Dallas asked.

He shook his head. "You mean no one ever told her where I was?"

Garrett let out a huff. "We've spent our whole lives trying to protect her from the kind of life you led. She already feels guilty enough for not being able to keep you with her. Even if we'd have known, I doubt we'd have made her feel any worse by telling her."

Jimmie rubbed his wrists where the handcuffs were pinching his skin. "I probably blew my chance to see her after today."

Garrett looked up at the guard. "The cuffs are too tight. I think we can loosen them a bit." The guard didn't move until Garrett and Dallas both showed their badges.

"She may chew you out, because she's your sister, but she'll probably come see you as soon as they let her out of the hospital."

He looked skeptical. "It's been more than twenty years."

"She's your sister, Jimmie, first and foremost. That shaped her entire life," Dallas said.

Garrett looked at him with surprise in his eyes. "Yeah, it did, didn't it?"

"Huh," Jimmie said, a puzzled look on his face. "I blamed her for a long time for leaving me with my uncle. Every time I said I missed her, I got a whoopin'. He told me she didn't want me, neither, nobody did, but I was his blood and burden."

Dallas glanced at Garrett. There was anger in both of their expressions. Garrett finally spoke up. "She cried for you, Jimmie. I heard her many nights. It wasn't her choice."

"She still misses you," Dallas added.

Garrett silently nodded.

"So she had a good life?" Jimmie asked.

"Yeah, pretty much." A smile twitched the corner of Garrett's mouth. "About as good as it gets for a girl with three older brothers. But she wasn't too spoiled. She works for social services now, trying to help kids like you and herself, kids who are going through the foster-care system. If we can arrange to keep you in Colorado long enough, she wants to see you."

Jimmie's leathery face brightened and tears welled in his eyes. "I'd like that, before I have to go back. I wanna tell her I'm sorry. And you, too. Real sorry."

"Time's up," the warden bellowed.

Jimmie stood, shuffling his feet. "You take good care of Kira, Dallas. I'm real sorry for hurting her."

"I'll tell her that, Jimmie," Dallas replied, struggling with his conflicting emotions. He'd never had much of a connection with a prisoner before. Not on the personal side, anyway.

Dallas and Garrett waited while the guard and Jimmie filed out of the room. "I see why Kira's so determined to help the kids now. You think she knew he was in prison?" Dallas asked.

"I didn't even know she was searching for him," Garrett said as he stood to leave. "I'll probably see you tomorrow."

Dallas stopped at the hospital to tell Kira what had happened. She'd fallen back to sleep, and her parents had gone home since Sorento was out of the picture now.

She had a peacefulness about her as she slept. Dallas was relieved for that.

"The doctor gave her a strong pain medication, Mr. Brooks, so she could sleep through the night. If you'd like to go home and get some rest, I'll call you when she's awake," a nurse told him.

"I'd really rather stay with her, if that's okay." He wasn't leaving until he'd told her about her brother and found out how soon she'd be released.

"I'll roll in a recliner for you, then," the nurse said with a smile.

Kira woke with pain shooting down her arm and aches from head to toe. She vaguely recalled what had happened and why she was here. She remembered Kent's visit, telling her that Sorento had arranged for her brother, Jimmie, to break out of prison.

She felt tears start again. *My own brother was sent to kill me,* she thought. *What a sick, sick man you were,*

Sorento. She blew her nose, then startled to see Dallas jump to his feet.

"What's wrong?" he said as he searched the room. "Kira, honey, are you okay?" He grabbed another box of tissues from the sink, pulled one from the box and gently wiped the tears from her face.

"Sorento," she sobbed, "got my brother out of prison…"

"I know. And he's never going to hurt you again. I talked to Jimmie last night. He said he's sorry for scaring us. He didn't know it was you, but he never planned to hurt anyone, especially not you." Dallas took hold of her hand. "He'd like to see you, if you're willing and we can work it out."

She was silent for a long time, wrestling with her tears. "This isn't exactly how I imagined seeing my brother again."

Dallas nodded, not rushing into platitudes just to make her feel better. She appreciated that. "It won't be easy for either of you. This time it will be a short visit, which may be best. You've grown up in different worlds, and it will take time to get to know each other."

She nodded, tears flowing. "He must have had a terrible upbringing with his uncle. He got into a lot of trouble."

"Yeah, but he'll have another chance. He's up for parole in a couple of years. A lot of people turn their lives around in prison, come out with a stronger grasp on life and a purpose. God didn't allow you two to find each other like this by coincidence. Maybe if Jimmie knows we're all going to be here for him, maybe he can realize his past is just that. I've overcome PTSD and you've overcome a difficult start in life. We'll get you through this, too. Together. And then Jimmie will be able to see that everyone has their hurdles in life. We just jump them one at a time. Let go of the past, and reach for what's in front of us. Let God handle the rest."

She raised a hand to his shirt and pulled him close. "I don't think I've said I love you today."

His eyes darted to the clock on the wall. "It's four in the morning, so no, I don't think you have," he whispered as he brushed a kiss across her forehead.

"I love you, Dallas, and I can't wait to be your wife."

He smiled and kissed the tip of her nose. "I—" he said as he kissed her chin "—love—" he kissed her earlobe "—you—" he paused and looked dreamily into her eyes "—too." Finally, his lips met hers. It was a kiss for her tired soul to melt into.

TWENTY-TWO

Three weeks later, Kira turned to watch Cody bringing Betsy up front for the children's sermon during church. As she did so, an incredibly handsome police officer sitting in the back pew caught her eye. Dallas looked surprisingly awake for someone just coming off a ten-hour shift. School was out and he was back on his street patrol for the summer. She'd begged him to get off early today, but he'd said no one was able to cover for him.

But he was here. He hurried up the aisle while the kids were filing up front, and slipped into the pew next to Kira. He smiled, and Kira felt herself relax just having him next to her.

So much had changed since the night they'd met. Betsy and Cody were happily settled in with the Woods family.

She'd seen her brother Jimmie, and though he was back in prison, they were getting to know each other again through letters.

She held on to a ray of hope not only for his future, but for hers, as well.

She slid her hand over to Dallas's and held it tight as the minister talked about God sending others to help when we need it most. He talked about helping others and learning to let others help us sometimes, too. A few minutes later his sermon got into a deeper discussion about finding unexpected blessings in our darkest hours. She felt at peace knowing that God had sent her Dallas.

Dallas focused on the minister, while his hand played with the diamond engagement ring he'd placed on Kira's finger just a few days earlier. She smiled, feeling the light of God's love pouring over them both.

Thank You for your bountiful blessings, Lord. For protecting us. For bringing Dallas into my life, opening my eyes to help me find the love of my life. And thank You for guiding us both as we go about our jobs. Teach us to follow your example in love, in forgiveness and in administering justice. Forgive me for thinking I can fix everything, and help me learn to turn to You first.

When the service was over, they stepped into the line of exiting parishioners next to her. "You didn't think I would make it this morning, did you?" Dallas asked.

"To be totally honest, no, I didn't. Did you hear them announce our engagement?" She longed to snuggle up to him, but rules were rules, after all, and he was still in uniform.

"I got here right before he announced it. I was

relieved that no one objected. How many more chances does the pastor give the congregation? I thought that was just at the wedding."

They were interrupted by the pastor's greeting. "Hello, I don't think we've formally met."

"Dallas Brooks, Kira's fiancé."

"It's nice to have you with us. I'm looking forward to getting to know you better," Pastor Stephenson added. "Morning, Kira. Are you both ready for our meeting this afternoon?"

The line was long this morning, and Kira didn't like to take too much time to chat. They'd have time later.

"One o'clock still work?" Dallas asked.

"That should be good," the pastor confirmed as he took hold of Kira's left hand, pausing to admire her engagement ring as he did. "The ring is almost as beautiful as the bride-to-be, isn't it, Dallas?"

"Not even close," Dallas said, his hand on Kira's waist.

"Wise man," the pastor said with a chuckle. "How is your shoulder doing, Kira?"

"Every day it's a little better," Kira said as she and Dallas walked out into the warm summer morning.

"So, you really think we can pass the pastor's muster?" Dallas asked.

"Of course," she said. "If you can pass my brothers' test, you've got nothing to worry about."

"How about if you give me a minute to change out of my uniform, and we'll go out for brunch?"

Kira smiled. "At a real restaurant, or…"

"I know, I know. Fast food doesn't qualify as a date. I meant to court you properly, Miss Matthews."

"Think you can really take four more months of this?" she teased.

"Piece of cake. I've got my eye on the prize," Dallas said with a smile. "Besides, who says the courtship has to end when we say 'I do'?"

* * * * *

Look for Nick Matthews's story,
BADGE OF HONOR,
coming in May 2008,
only from Love Inspired Suspense.

Dear Reader,

So many times in our lives, it feels as if life hits us from every direction, all at once. Sometimes it's hard for us to catch our breath. Sometimes God's plan for our lives forces us to stretch ourselves outside our comfort zone. I know that His intention is to show me, as many times as necessary, that He is always there to guide me and to be my everything.

In today's world, it isn't easy to find a way to slow down, to accept our limitations and still be obedient to God, our families and our responsibilities. Kira and Dallas have a lifetime of baggage—as we all do—that they need to learn how to manage. How they deal with those challenges is unique for each of them, because God created them to complement one another.

I hope you will enjoy reading about the journey these two go through as they try to figure out how to do their jobs, understand God's plan for them and balance that with their feelings about each other. If you have time to write, I'd love to hear from you about how God carries you through the tough times. You can e-mail me at csteward37@aol.com or P.O. Box 200286, Evans, CO 80620.

Sincerely,

Carol Steward

QUESTIONS FOR DISCUSSION

1. Dallas experienced post-traumatic stress after a shooting on the job. Have you ever experienced post-traumatic stress? What happened? How did you deal with it?

2 Kira grew up in a law-enforcement family, yet chose to become a social worker. Do you think her parents were disappointed that she chose social work? Did you ever choose a different path from your family's? If so, what happened?

3 Dallas is not happy when he's asked to fill in for a school security officer at a local high school. Does he handle things well? What would you have done in his place?

4. After the arrest at the beginning of the book, Dallas is concerned about Kira's safety and wants to make sure she's all right. Is this appropriate, considering they hardly knew each other? Discuss why or why not.

5. The real world sometimes places a brick wall in the way of idealism. How does Kira maintain her positive attitude with all that happens to her?

6. Kira went into social services because of her troubled childhood. How does her past give her insight into the lives of the children she helps now? Does your past help you with your present life?

7. Torn from her brother at a young age, Kira has been trying to find him for twenty years. How do you think she feels when she discovers he's been involved with criminals? How you ever been disappointed by the truth? How did you deal with it?

8. After Dallas tells Kira about his post-traumatic stress disorder, he lets her—and God—into his heart. What is it about telling the truth that opens us up to love? Discuss a time when this happened to you.

9. Dallas and Kira discover that criminals in their small town are making and dealing illegal drugs. Were you surprised by this? Why or why not? Have you come across this in your town or city?

10. Not much is made of the fact that Kira is biracial, and was adopted by a white family. Do you know any families who have adopted outside their race or nationality? What problems do you think they encounter?

LOVE INSPIRED HISTORICAL
*Powerful, engaging stories of romance, adventure and
faith set the in the past—when life was simpler and
faith played a major role in everyday lives.*

Turn the page for a sneak preview of
THE BRITON
By
Catherine Palmer

*Love Inspired Historical—love and faith
throughout the ages
A brand-new line from Steeple Hill Books
Launching this February!*

"Welcome to the family, Briton," said one of Olaf's men in a mocking voice. "We look forward to the presence of a woman at our hall."

Bronwen grasped her tunic and yanked it from the Viking's thick fingers. As she stepped away from the table, she heard the drunken laughter of the barbarians behind her. How could her father have betrothed her to the old Viking?

Running down the steps toward the heavy oak door that led outside the keep, Bronwen gathered her mantle about her. She ordered the doorman to open it, and he did so reluctantly, pressing her to carry a torch. But Bronwen pushed past him and fled into the darkness.

Dashing down the steep, pebbled hill toward the beach, she felt the frozen ground give way to sand. She threw off her veil and circlet and kicked away her shoes.

Racing alongside the pounding surf, she felt hot tears of anger and shame well up and stream down her cheeks. With no concern for her safety, Bronwen ran and ran, her long braids streaming behind her, falling loose, drifting like a tattered black flag.

Blinded with weeping, she did not see the dark form that loomed suddenly in her path and stopped dead her headlong sprint. Bronwen shrieked in surprise and fear as iron arms pinned her, and a heavy cloak threatened to suffocate her.

"Release me!" she cried. "Guard! Guard, help me!"

"Hush, my lady." A deep voice emanated from the darkness. "I mean you no harm. What demon drives you to run so madly in the night without fear for your safety?"

"Release me, villain! I am the daughter—"

"I shall hold you until you calm yourself. We had heard there were witches in Amounderness, but I had not thought to meet one so openly."

Still held tight in the man's arms, Bronwen drew back and peered up at the hooded figure. "You! You are the man who spied on our feast. Release me at once, or I shall call the guard upon you."

The man chuckled at this and turned toward his companions, who stood in a group nearby. Bronwen caught hold of the back of his hood and jerked it down to reveal a head of glossy raven curls. But the man's face was shrouded in darkness yet, and as he looked at her, she could not read his expression.

"So you are the blessed bride-to-be." He pulled the

hood back over his head. "Your father has paired you with an interesting choice."

Relieved that her captor did not appear to be a high-wayman, she sagged from his warm hands onto the wet sand. "Please leave me here alone. I need peace to think. Go on your way."

The tall stranger shrugged off his outer mantle and wrapped it around her shoulders. "Why did your father betroth you thus to the aged Viking?" he asked.

For one purported to be a spy, you know precious little about Amounderness. But I shall tell you, as it is all common knowledge."

She pulled the cloak tightly about her, reveling in its warmth. "Our land, Amounderness, once was Briton territory. Olaf Lothbrok, my betrothed, came here as a youth when the Viking invasions had nearly subsided. He took the lands directly to the south of Rossall Hall from their Briton lord. Then, of course, the Normans came, and Amounderness was pillaged by William the Conqueror's army."

The man squatted on the sand beside Bronwen. He listened with obvious interest as she continued the familiar tale. "When William took an account of Amounderness in his Domesday Book, he recorded no remaining lords and few people at all. But he did not know the Britons. Slowly we crept out of hiding and returned to our halls. My father's family reoccupied Rossall Hall. And there we live, as we should, watching over our serfs as they fish and grow their meager crops. Indeed, there is not much here for the greedy Normans to want, if they are the ones for whom you spy."

Unwilling to continue speaking when her heart was to heavy, Bronwen stood and turned toward the sea. The traveler rose beside her and touched her arm. "Olaf Lothbrok's lands—together with your father's—will reunite most of Amounderness. A clever plan. You sister's future husband holds the rest of the adjoining lands, I understand."

"You've done your work, sir. Your lord will be pleased. Who is he—some land-hungry Scottish baron? Or have you forgotten that King Stephen gave Amounderness to the Scots as a trade for their support in his war with Matilda? I certainly hope your lord is not a Norman. He would be so disappointed to learn he has not legal rights here. Now, if you will excuse me?"

Bronwen turned and began walking back along the beach toward Rosall Hall. She felt better for her run, and somehow her father's plan did not seem so far-fetched anymore. Distant lights twinkled through the fog that was rolling in from the west, and she suddenly realized what a long way she had come.

"My lady," the stranger's voice called out behind her.

Bronwen kept walking, unwilling to face again the one who had seen her in her humiliation. She did not care what he reported to his master.

"My lady, you have a bit of a walk ahead of you." The

traveler strode forward to join her. "Perhaps I should accompany you to your destination."

"You leave me no choice, I see."

"I am not one to compromise myself, dear lady. I follow the path God has set before me and none other."

"And just who are you?"

"I am called Jacques."

"French. A Norman, as I had suspected."

The man chuckled. "Not nearly as Norman as you are Briton."

As they approached the fortress, Bronwen could see that the guests had not yet begun to disperse. Perhaps no one had missed her, and she could slip quietly into bed beside Gildan.

She turned to go, but he took her arm and studied her face in the moonlight. Then, gently, he drew her into the folds of his hooded cloak. "Perhaps the bride would like the memory of a younger man's embrace to warm her," he whispered.

Astonished, Bronwen attempted to remove his arms from around her waist. But she could not escape his lips as they found her own. The kiss was soft and warm, melting away her resistance like the sun upon the snow. Before she had time to react, he was striding back down the beach.

Bronwen stood stunned for a moment, clutching his woollen mantle about her. Suddenly she cried out, "Wait, Jacques! Your mantle!"

The dark one turned to her. "Keep it for now," he shouted into the wind. "I shall ask for it when we meet again."

* * * * *

Don't miss this deeply moving
Love Inspired Historical story about
a medieval lady who finds strength in God
to save her family legacy—and to open her heart to love.

THE BRITON
by Catherine Palmer
available February 2008

And also look for
HOMESPUN BRIDE
by Jillian Hart,
where a Montana woman discovered that love
is the greatest blessing of all.

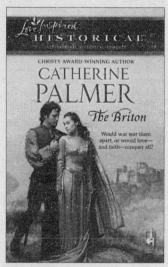

REQUEST YOUR FREE BOOKS!
2 FREE RIVETING INSPIRATIONAL NOVELS PLUS 2 FREE MYSTERY GIFTS

YES! Please send me 2 FREE Love Inspired® Suspense novels and my 2 FREE mystery gifts. After receiving them, if I don't wish to receive any more books, I can return the shipping statement marked "cancel." If I don't cancel, I will receive 4 brand-new novels every month and be billed just $3.99 per book in the U.S. or $4.74 per book in Canada, plus 25¢ shipping and handling per book and applicable taxes, if any*. That's a savings of 20% off the cover price! I understand that accepting the 2 free books and gifts places me under no obligation to buy anything. I can always return a shipment and cancel at any time. Even if I never buy another book from Steeple Hill, the two free books and gifts are mine to keep forever.

123 IDN EL5H 323 IDN ELQH

Name	(PLEASE PRINT)	
Address		Apt. #
City	State/Prov.	Zip/Postal Code
Signature (if under 18, a parent or guardian must sign)		

Order online at www.LoveInspiredSuspense.com

Or mail to Steeple Hill Reader Service™:

IN U.S.A.: P.O. Box 1867, Buffalo, NY 14240-1867
IN CANADA: P.O. Box 609, Fort Erie, Ontario L2A 5X3

Not valid to current Love Inspired Suspense subscribers.

Want to try two free books from another series?
Call 1-800-873-8635 or visit www.morefreebooks.com

* Terms and prices subject to change without notice. NY residents add applicable sales tax. Canadian residents will be charged applicable provincial taxes and GST. This offer is limited to one order per household. All orders subject to approval. Credit or debit balances in a customer's account(s) may be offset by any other outstanding balance owed by or to the customer. Please allow 4 to 6 weeks for delivery.

Your Privacy: Steeple Hill is committed to protecting your privacy. Our Privacy Policy is available online at www.eHarlequin.com or upon request from the Reader Service. From time to time we make our lists of customers available to reputable firms who may have a product or service of interest to you. If you would prefer we not share your name and address, please check here. ☐

Love Inspired
SUSPENSE

TITLES AVAILABLE NEXT MONTH

Don't miss these four stories in February

VENDETTA by Roxanne Rustand
Snow Canyon Ranch

After what the McAllisters did to his father, Cole Daniels was
determined never to forgive or forget. Then Leigh McAllister
landed in danger, and Cole had to decide what was stronger–
his old grudge or his need to protect his new chance at love.

MISSING PERSONS by Shirlee McCoy
Reunion Revelations

Lauren Owens had her job and her faith on track, and she
looked forward to tackling the mystery back at Magnolia
College...until the problem turned deadly. She found herself
turning to ex-boyfriend Seth Chartrand for support, for
safety and love.

BAYOU CORRUPTION by Robin Caroll

All Alyssa LeBlanc wanted was to distance herself
from Lagniappe, Louisiana...and from ace reporter
Jackson Devereaux. But once she witnessed the attack on
the sheriff, she knew she couldn't walk away. Working with
Jackson, Alyssa investigated the crime–and uncovered her
past.

LETHAL DECEPTION by Lynette Eason

When guerillas held Cassidy McKnight captive in the Amazon,
ex-Navy SEAL turned E.R. doctor Gabe Sinclair returned to
his military roots to rescue her. He thought the job was done,
yet danger followed Cassidy home....

LISCNM0108